MOB LIFE

ADDICTED TO HIS LOVE

CHANIQUE' J.

MOB Life

Copyright © 2018 by Chanique' J.

Published by Shan Presents
www.shanpresents.com

This is a work of fiction. Any references or similarities to actual events, real people, living or dead, or to the real locals intended to give the novel a sense of reality. Any similarity in other names, characters, places, and incidents are entirely coincidental.

SUBSCRIBE

Text Shan to 22828 to stay up to date with new releases, sneak peeks, contest, and more....

WANT TO BE A PART OF SHAN PRESENTS?

To submit your manuscript to Shan Presents, please send the first three chapters and synopsis to submissions@shanpresents.com

MOB LIFE:

ADDICTED TO HIS LOVE

By:
Chaniqué J.

ACKNOWLEDGMENTS

As always, I want to thank God first, who is the reason I am able to complete book after book. This journey has been nothing short of amazing. From my very first book two years ago, up until my latest release, I learn a little more every step of the way.

I want to give my adorable son Ke-Chan a shout out for being my sunshine through my rainy days!

Family, of course, I want to thank each and every one of you! I hate this part because I always feel like someone is left out, but not intentionally.

Friends and supporters, you guys are amazing, and I consider you all my extended family. The motivation and drive I receive from you all is phenomenal.

My Pen sisters and Publisher Shan, thanks for always supporting me and helping when in need. Short and sweet is what I wanted the acknowledgments for my 18th book to be, so I'm ending this here. Go ahead and enjoy what book 18 has to offer and stay tuned for part two.

Sincerely, Chanique J.

SYNOPSIS

Connected by fate and not by luck is the code these three sisters live by. Deja, Dreia, and Destini were just living their best lives without a care in the world, until each of them had their heart captured by one of the Jones' Brothers. For Romeo, Julian, and Omar, love wasn't in their future; it was always money and drugs over everything. No one had time to catch feelings and put it all on the line. One thing for sure, the couples weren't prepared for the troubles that awaited. Take this journey with these three couples to see how this MOB love story unfolds.

ONE

DEJA

I couldn't get out of that club fast enough, it seems like happy hour on Friday is always super busy. You would think a celebrity was in the building or something. We had a full house from the time I walked in this afternoon. Don't get me wrong, I love the money, and the fact that it's a fast-paced environment. But I had shit I needed to do today. I had hopes of sneaking out early so I could finish getting my shit together for the All-White event tonight.

Working as a club promoter and bartender has its perks, because I'm always up on game when it comes to the upcoming events. I'm not talking some small club event with a crowd of a hundred people or less, either. I'm talking the top paid people of the city. You know, like the boss's boss. I'm not the richest bitch walking around, but I damn sure ain't broke either. I refuse to party with those who are in the same tax bracket as I'm in. Even at the young age of twenty-three, I know in order to become a boss and live the lifestyle that I want, I gotta surround myself with those who have what I desire out of life. This All-White event I plan on attending is one of the biggest events in the city. Everybody in the city wants to attend this event, but not everyone will be making the cut. You had to either be in good acquaintance with someone who is hosting the party, or on the very strict guest list. Thank goodness for the connects of being a high-end event promoter, I was able to make that guest list without any efforts, along with my two sisters.

I'm on that Henny, I'm on that X
Ima fuck yo bitch out her heel, heel, heels (Pop!)
Pill Popper (Pop!)
Seal- Popper (Woah!)

Coasting on the highway in the direction of Oohs & Ahs hair salon, *Hip Hopper* by Blac Youngsta Feat Lil Yachty filled the speakers of my 2016 all white Chevy Malibu. Just hearing this beat made me want to start fucking it up right here in my front seat. Thank goodness traffic wasn't bad, for it to be a little after four o'clock on a Friday. I had already planned on making it to my appointment about fifteen minutes late, but fortunately, time is on my side today and I'll be there just in time. Yesterday I had gotten a balance for my nails, pedicure, and a silk press by the best, Shea, so my hair wasn't the issue. But these brows and lashes, on the other hand, were in dire need of a touch-up. Shea also does my brows and lashes, so if I need a touch up on my hair, I could do so. I try to keep my brows maintained at least once a week, just because a pretty chick like me can't be seen looking just any old kind of way. I have a reputation to uphold. I see too many people a day to get caught slipping.

When I walked into the shop, it was jammed packed. I don't know why I would expect anything less, considering it's a Friday. All the hoes were trying to get dolled up, so they could hit somebody's club scene this weekend. On top of it being Friday, it's the first Friday of the month, so some bitches got their welfare checks and their poor babies' funds were going directly towards the mommas' weekend agendas. Thank goodness for being a regular and having a scheduled appointment, I was able to walk in and sit right in Shea's chair. Shea knew how serious I was when it came to my appearance. After a quick thirty minutes, I was walking out the door just as fast as I walked in.

Before I could head home just yet, I needed to make a quick run to the mall and grab a clutch to match my pumps for tonight. Unfortunately, I had to go all the way across town to the mall because the one by the hair salon is trash. Eastland Mall has gone to hell over the years. It's almost like a damn flea market now. So Polaris was the best bet if I planned on finding something worth my while. I was able to find the perfect gold pumps in Aldo, to set off my all white skin-tight dress for the evening, earlier this week. The clutch I originally wanted I saw online and there was no way I could order and receive it by today, so I had to find something similar. I was hoping like hell that Macy's or Saks would have just what I needed.

I was able to find a parking spot right in front of Saks, and no sooner than I walked into the doors, I saw the display of purses. There was a Gold crystal-like clutch that caught my eye from a distance. I knew it was just what I was looking for. Now, the catch was the fucking price. Just as I expected, they wanted damn near three hundred dollars for a fucking clutch. Two hundred and eighty-four dollars for a clutch was a bit much, but I didn't have the time to look around anymore only to end up finding nothing else. My damn dress ain't even cost that much. I was able to luck up and find one for only sixty dollars on Fashion Nova's website. *Fuck it, YOLO,* I thought to myself and motioned for the sales lady to come unhook the clutch, so I could be on my merry little way.

Last stop before I could head home and unwind was the liquor store. I, for sure, needed to pregame before I headed out. Now don't get it twisted, I'm no drunk. But considering I work around liquor all day every day, Patrón and a shot of Sprite are two of my closest friends. Besides, I needed to grab a pack of Swishers. Dreia was at home waiting for me to bring them to her, she wasn't a big drinker, but she did smoke weed. For the most part, she eats edibles, but those are two completely different highs.

"Hunny, I'm home!" I yelled out, greeting Dreia.

"Hunny I'm home, my ass. You took long enough. Where is my shells?" Dreia yelled back from upstairs.

"Don't even trip, I got your shit. I had to stop by Saks and grab this clutch to go with my outfit for tonight, that's what took so long. Damn, I mean you could've easily got off your ass and went to get your own shells without the wait." I joked with her.

"Now why would I do such a thing when my doll face would have to stop on the way home anyway?" she replied sarcastically. Just as I expected, when I walked up the stairs she was lounging in her room across the bed with only her bra and panties on. I know she probably had been that way since she got home and would continue to sit around like such until it was time to get dressed for the party.

"Let me guess, you waiting for your package to arrive still?" I asked, referring to her sack of loud her little boo thing was supposed to be dropping off to her.

"And you know this. I swear niggas don't have a sense of urgency to save their lives. I mean, I ain't complaining too much cause I ain't paying for the shit. Plus, you just got here, but damn." Dreia said.

"Right, you can't be too demanding when you're getting the shit for free and always do. Now, if you were a paying customer, that would be another story. He only taking his time because he probably gone try to convince your ass to stay in tonight and not step out with us."

"Yeah, he can try that shit if he wants to, but I'm not goin'. I'm sure he will be in attendance, so why can't I be? It's not like we together anymore, anyways. Shit, I need to get out and see what I been missing out on."

Dreia was now up on her feet getting dressed. The outfit she picked out for tonight fit her perfectly. It's been so long since I saw her show some damn skin in public, I was hella excited.

"Bihhh please, zaddy ain't playing that. I don't know who the hell you trying to convince, me or yourself, cause we all know he ain't going for you talking to nobody at that damn party if he is there. He is going to be hot on your heels. Especially with the way that ass sitting up in your romper."

"Yesss! I can't wait to step out, it's long overdue. Have you talked to Destini to see if she was going to pick us up or if we needed to meet her at her place?"

"No, I haven't talked to her since before I went to work earlier today. I'm sure her mean ass probably going to say come to her place since she's already driving."

"You right, but I'm going send her as a text just to be sure anyway" Dreia said as the doorbell chimed, alerting us of a guest. I wasn't expecting anyone, so I walked to my room to prepare myself for the evening. Dreia could grab the door since it's her company.

WHEN WE PULLED up the location that the party was being hosted, I was in awe. The size of this house reminded me of something I would see in a magazine. It had to be no less than fifteen thousand square feet, and I'm only referring to the house. The outside was a European Country style build. There was a waterfall in the center of the circular driveway near the double entrance doors of the house. There were several stone statues of different figures in the yard leading up to the entrance. This house made the mini-mansion we grew up in look like a fucking shack.

We didn't grow up with silver spoons in our mouths, but our foster mother Maris wasn't broke, either. She made sure we had the things we needed, and the things we wanted we had to work for. She reminded us daily that money could cause a person to lose all humbleness and she didn't want that for any of us. Granted our home was nice and the cars she drove were nice, we were still looked upon as being average girls growing up. I knew the Jones brothers had a couple coins, but damn. If they were doing it like this just for a place to host their party, I could only imagine how they were really living.

I've never been the groupie type, but I see how bitches falls in love with the money before they fall in love with the nigga.

Valet members came to all doors of the car and helped us out. All three of our feet hit the pavement and our appearance fit in perfectly with those surrounding us. Looking like three million bucks, we headed in the direction of the doormen, so we could get inside. With every step I took, I could feel my dress rising, but that was the purpose. I wanted to show something, not too much, but just enough for the looking eyes. The dress was just a plain sleeveless V-neck, with a low backdrop, but the way it fit every curve of my body it didn't matter just how plain it really was. I accessorized the hell out of it with my gemmed-out clutch, pumps, and diamond choker. I wasn't for all the costume jewelry tonight, so I wore a simple diamond bracelet, a pair of diamond studded earrings to match my choker, since my hair would be covering my ears anyway, there was no point in wearing anything dramatic, and a diamond ring on my left hand.

Destini gave the doorman our names, and without any hassle, he located our names on the guest list and allowed us access to the party. The music couldn't be heard outside, but the moment we stepped foot in the house, you could hear Moneybagg Yo feat. Yo Gotti's *Reflection* booming through the surround sound speakers. There were so many people walking around with drinks in their hands and smiles on their faces. You could tell we were surrounded by money when it came to the men. Now the women, on the other hand, I could spot a few hood rats that slid through the cracks somehow, some way. But I guess a party ain't a party without a few ratchets being present.

Destini told us she would be back and headed on her own way. Destini's all white ankle length dress was so bomb. The way it flowed as she walked looked like something you would see on a model in a magazine. I loved how classy my sister dressed, you would never know just how hood she is just off her appearance. Dreia was already high, so she was in her zone. I needed to head to wherever the drinks were. Following the marble floors to the rear of the house, we landed on the exit towards the backyard. There was a huge Olympic size pool that was lit up with different neon lights. A few females had their feet in the water while a few others were in their bathing suits. Shit! Not I! There was no way in hell you would catch me dead in the pool at this party. I came to sit pretty and enjoy myself, not work out and ruin the silk press I just got. My hair is natural and a drop of water will result in shrinkage out of this world. Besides, the way my natural hair was flowing down the drop in the middle of my dress in the back was a damn good look.

"Can I help you ladies with something to drink?" A waiter asked us with a tray of various cups.

"Yes, do you have Patrón?" I asked while eyeing over the several cups that were neatly placed on the drink tray.

"Yes. How about for you ma'am?" the waiter asked Dreia.

"Oh, no thank you!" she replied. I slightly nudged her because she could order one for me, just so I wouldn't have to wait until the next waiter came around when I wanted another cup.

"Then again I'll take the same thing please."

The waiter smiled and handed us both our drinks.

"Thank you!" we both said in unison.

I took the first cup to the head, in the most ladylike manner possible, and headed over to where I noticed a couple of empty seats. When we sat down, I was able to look around and admire the beautiful set up of the backyard. Although there was a full party going on, you could still tell how immaculate this place actually was. There were tents set up throughout the yard along with a DJ booth. Amongst the guests of the party, we were able to identify several waiters and waitresses some serving full meals, while others were serving other refreshments, such as light finger foods and non-alcoholic beverages. The DJ that was outside was on the same track as the one inside, making it appear as if it was the same person on the ones and twos. I found that to be pretty unique. Normally, when there is more than one DJ, they played separate tracks, but not these two.

Dreia and I remained seated talking while in the midst of the crowds of people walking around the party. Dreia must have been feeling some type of way because she even had her a shot of Patrón. She's normally not big on alcohol, but I'm sure it was because she noticed her little boo hadn't hit her up so that only meant he was somewhere in here enjoying himself. There were more than enough bitches to go around, so I'm sure he was entertained. It's not like this was the type of party where I would get up and started twerking or anything, so I just continued to sit and sip. Thank goodness the waiters were on top of their shit, because they continued to come around and offer drinks. As long as they offered, I would kindly accept. My tolerance is really high, but I still planned on taking it easy, so I wouldn't be too drunk.

I noticed the chick who was just in the pool screaming for attention from her behaviors, was now out of the water and walking towards our direction with the biggest grin on her face. She looked as if she was a kid in the candy store and I couldn't fathom why, until I heard Dreia say, "There's Romeo, the youngest Jones brother."

Looking over my shoulder, I saw him walking in our direction. I couldn't tell if he was walking towards our table or the woman on the opposite side of us, heading in his direction.

"Zam Zaddy, I've been looking all over for you!" the short light-skinned chick said to Romeo as she reached for his embrace and he shot that shit down. She had to have been drunk if she even thought twice about him hugging her soaking wet and he was dressed in all white, Cocaine Crazy as I would call it, looking good enough to eat.

"You couldn't have been looking that hard if you are soaking wet. Cause you know for damn sure I wasn't getting in no water." Romeo replied to her nonchalantly while looking past her in our direction.

"I mean, I was looking before I decided to dive in and enjoy the pool. That's is the purpose of the pool being out here." she said in her defense.

"You right, but nah I just got here actually not too long ago. From the looks of it, you're enjoying yourself though right." he said to her.

"Yes, but I'm enjoying myself even more now that I got the chance to see you." This chick was sounding and looking beyond pressed, and he wasn't even biting the bait she was delivering. Poor little tink tink just doesn't know how bad she looked from another bitch's point of view. The moment he looked over my shoulder and didn't make eye contact with me, I would've ended the conversation.

"I'm glad I could do that for you! Go ahead and finish enjoying the amenities the pool has to offer and I'll get up with you a little later. I'm about to mingle a little." Romeo said and walked right past the girl in route to where Dreia and I were seated.

I don't know if it was the Patrón having an effect on me or just his presence, but I felt the moisture between my legs begin to increase. I had the opportunity to see Romeo on several occasions, but never on a personal type of level. Up close, in person, with the addition of liquor, he was looking mighty tasty, but I wouldn't let him know that. Dreia pulled her blunt from her wristlet and lit it as he walked over and took a seat across from me.

"How y'all ladies doing tonight?" Romeo asked with a smile that was worth looking at all night.

"Good, how about yourself?" Dreia asked in between exhaling her smoke. I hadn't even noticed she lit up a blunt we pre-rolled before coming to the party.

"I'm well, thanks for askin'." I replied.

"I'm aight. Can I get y'all anything? Are y'all enjoying this little shit?" he questioned, downplaying this party as if it wasn't one of the biggest events of the year.

"We good, y'all got hella help around here tending to the guests." I replied while reaching for my cup of Patrón. I lost count after the first few cups, honestly.

"The only thing you can help me with is pointing in what direction is the ladies room," Dreia questioned. Romeo raised his arm slightly and within seconds there was a waitress on the side of him at his command.

"Aye Miss Lady, can you be so kind to show..." Romeo took a break and Dreia filled in the blank he was looking for.

"Dreia, my name is Dreia."

"Thank you." he replied. "Can you show Dreia to the ladies' room, please?"

"No problem. Right this way, follow me," the nice waitress responded.

"I'm sorry I didn't introduce myself. I'm Romeo, and you are?"

"Hello Romeo, I'm Dej." I greeted him as if I didn't know who he was prior to him introducing himself. I mean, who wouldn't know who he was? Romeo is only one of the most well-known niggas in our city.

"Dej, like short for what Deja?" he questions with that same smile on his face.

"Yeah, but everyone calls me Dej."

Romeo just didn't know how memorizing his eye contact was. I had to keep taking small sips of my drink, so I wouldn't become hypnotized by his trance.

"Dej short for Deja, huh?" he said while rubbing his beard as if he really was thinking about my name. "Deja fits you well, I don't think I've had the pleasure of ever seeing you around, Deja. Are you from here?"

"Yeah, born and raised." I was trying to keep it short because I'm sure my words would be slurred if I said any more than a few words. I didn't want to appear to be drunk and unable to handle my liquor. Romeo's phone went off as I noticed Dreia heading back in our direction.

"Aight, I'll be right there. Give me a second, I'm out in the back." Romeo spoke into his phone with so much authority.

"I'm sorry about that Ms. Deja, I'm sorry Dej. Can I have your number, so we can finish the conversation? I'd hate to just stop right there when we were just getting acquainted."

No sooner than he completed his sentence, Dreia took her seat and the light-skinned chick that was in his face minutes earlier was standing beside him grabbing his shoulder in a seductive manner, as if she was letting it be known she had some sort of tab on him. Little did she know I wasn't checking for this nigga. He was sexy as shit, but I knew exactly what came with the money, fame, and looks of a Jones brother, and I didn't need nor want any parts of that bullshit.

"I'm sure this won't be the last time we see each other. It was a pleasure meeting you as well." I said, not only shutting him down, but ending our conversation right then and there before he could go any further, and either embarrassed himself or the chick standing beside him.

"Bet, you got it. Alright, Dreia and Deja, y'all enjoy yourselves and don't have too much fun," Romeo said while standing to his feet and walking away with the chick on the heel of his white Giuseppe sneakers. If I didn't know any better, I would think they were fucking currently on the low, or have fucked before, just by the way she was on him.

"Was it just me or was baby girl on it with Romeo? She came over here making sure her territory was covered." Dreia said while laughing.

"Bihhh, I was thinking the same thing. Little did she know he was checking for me, not the other way around. I ain't got time for the flock of groupies or fans that come with that man and his money."

"I hear you, but I also noticed how you eyed him. You can fool her and him, but I know when you are feeling somebody." Dreia was right, but damn she ain't have to call it like that.

"I can't lie, baby Issa Snack, but just not for me." I joked back with her.

The remainder of the evening, we walked around a little to see just what the rest of the house looked like and to see the faces of the other guests. We had yet still to cross paths with Kamar, Dreia's boo thang. I could tell she wanted to at least for him to see her and how good she was looking in her all-white romper with the red accessories. The red bottoms she was rocking helped to set off her outfit just right. Shit, I wanted for him to see her too, because he needed to see just how good she was looking and how many niggas were eyeing her, when she kept running back and forth with him.

Destini had sent us a few text messages checking on us

throughout the night, but we hadn't run back into her since we walked in. Ain't no telling where she had ventured off to. One thing we knew was that she could hold her own, and we didn't have any enemies to be worried about, so there were no worries because we would link when it was time to leave.

Inside was where the real partying was going on. You would've thought it was the club scene by the way people were dancing and turning up. The outside section must have been for the more laid-back crowd. It was for sure jumping in the house. Made me want to turn up with them, but I had few too many drinks to even try it. I even noticed a few females had removed their heels and were down-right twerking like they were at a freak neak contest. Of course, we were doing our own little two-step, but that was home for us. Nothing more, nothing less.

"Damn, I ain't seen nothing this enticing since I walked in this bitch." I heard a male voice say coming from the side of us. I looked over and I'll be damned if it wasn't another Jones brother. You could definitely tell that they were siblings, because they all have a very strong resemblance. Dreia looked over in his direction and continued on doing her two-step like he wasn't just eye fucking her while licking his lips.

"Aye, can I talk to you for a second?" the brother, I believe was Julian, asked Dreia while reaching out for her hand.

Dreia was a little hesitant about giving him her hand and step-ping to the side to talk to him, but she did. She was probably scared that Kamar would finally appear out of nowhere and catch her enter-taining another nigga. But last I checked, they were both single. I'm sure he was in here somewhere entertaining a couple of females. So why shouldn't she entertain one of the hosts of the party?

As bad as my drunk ass wanted to ear hustle and see what type of shit he was spitting to her, I couldn't hear them over the music. By the time the chopped it up a few minutes, Destini was heading in our direction.

"I been texting you, Dej." Destini said when she made it over to us.

"Have you? My damn phone in my clutch and we been in this bitch enjoying the party. I didn't even feel it vibrating, my fault."

"It's coo, I was just seeing if y'all were ready to head out. It's damn near three."

I reached into my clutch and retrieved my phone. I'll be damned if it was that late and I hadn't even realized it. I guess time flies when you're having fun, cause it didn't even feel like it was that late.

"I'm coo with that. I gotta work tomorrow anyway." Dreia said. I had to work too, but I was about this nightlife. Partying is part of my job description, so I'm used to it.

"It doesn't matter to me, I'm done drinking for the night. One more drink and y'all gone have to escort me out this bitch cause I'm holding on by a thread." I said to them honestly and we all started laughing.

They both knew just how wasted I could get in the blink of an eye. I was doing good by holding it together this long. Being the youngest, they always expected that type of shit outta me though, so they never tripped on my wild ways.

Heading out, valet already had Destini's car waiting for us at the door. *Now that's the shit I like to see,* I thought to myself. Just like the valet had done when we arrived, three gentlemen opened the car doors for us and assisted with us getting into her car. Lawd knows I needed the help, because when I landed in that back seat, I was letting loose. As soon as the doors were closed, I removed my pumps so fast. I had been walking around in them damn six-inch heels like they were sneakers. I looked to my right out the window and noticed Romeo was walking in the direction of the car, but he was a little too late. He gave me what appeared to be a wink and a head nod. Something told me this wouldn't be the last of this nigga, and a part of me was ok with that.

TWO

ROMEO

I don't give a fuck what shawty said, I know she was feeling the kid, no matter how hard to get she was playing. Surprisingly, I had never crossed paths with little miss Deja before, that alone let me know she wasn't one of these typical hood rats. Had she been one of them, I would've already smashed. It's not too many cute thottys I haven't touched. I'm not bragging or nothing, but I've had my fair share of women at my young age of twenty-five.

When I noticed her sitting over there with her friend, I had to go introduce myself. Had I known that Shadeia would be on my trail cock blocking, I would've waited to shoot my shot, but it is what it is. Trust me when I say, what I want, I get when I say I'm going to get Miss Deja. Shadeia and I fucked around from time-to-time, but it was never anything serious, and I don't know why she couldn't get that through her fucking skull. Whenever we see each other out and about, it's like she has to make it known that she's on it with me. That shit is annoying as fuck. No nigga wants no groupie trying to scare off other females if it's nothing between them.

Shadeia knows damn well she ain't my lady and will never be. I can't wife no thot ass bitch like her. I hit that shit the first night. We grown, so there's nothing wrong with fucking on the first night. But when you throw the pussy the first night and swallow my kids too, I can't get down like that. Shit, who's to say she don't do that to every nigga she crosses paths with. Prime example why I haven't wifed a bitch to this point. Well, that and the fact that I'm only twenty-five. I'm not sure if I'm ready to wife anyone just yet. I got a lot of life to live and a lot of shit to experience before I decide to dedicate myself to one female.

I noticed Deja and her friend leaving the party and I tried my hardest to get to her before they got in the car, but I was stopped by one of the party promoters about some cash. It was business, or else I would've had the nigga wait until I got finished talking to shawty. The look on her face when she noticed me walkin in her direction was of pure bliss. Deja knew what she was doing, but like she said, I'm sure we will cross paths again. The only thing with that is, I'm going to have to do my research on her, because we had never crossed paths before. So more than likely, we wouldn't just randomly cross paths in the future.

Shortly after Deja and her friend left the party it was over anyway, so I hopped in my fully loaded 2018 Chevy Camaro headed in the direction of my home. As bad as I wanted some pussy tonight, I ain't want none of the bitches I had been fucking around with. Shadeia hit my line a couple of times, but I let that shit go straight to voicemail. She needed to learn a lesson about her clingy ass behavior and her punishment would be restriction until further notice. Then, when I do finally decide to break her ass off again, I'm goin to set her straight on her behavior in public when we run into each other.

I hadn't realized just how fucked up I was until I stepped foot into my crib. The moment I sat on the cream-colored Bradley leather sectional in my living room, it was lights out. Had my phone not continued to go off, I probably would've remained sleep there on the couch in my living room.

"Yo, what's up?" I groggily answered the phone.

"Nigga, how long you plan on playing sleeping beauty? We got shit to do and your ass over there in a slumber like a pretty little princess." Julian said.

"Fuck you nigga, it's still early. What the fuck are you talking about? You the only muthafucka that gets up before the sun rises and expects niggas to be on the same shit as you."

"Fuck is you talking about, nigga? It's damn near 1 o'clock in the afternoon." Julian responded. I took the phone away from my ear to confirm if what he was saying was correct and I'll be damned if it wasn't twelve fifty in the afternoon.

"Shit, I ain't even realize it was that late. The fuck was in the damn shots of Patrón? A nigga ain't never slept this late on a Saturday. I'm bout to hop in the shower and I'll meet you at The Slab." The slab is our pops' home. We've been referring to it as The Slab since we were young niggas.

"Bet and hurry the fuck up nigga." Julian said before ending the call.

I immediately hopped up and headed upstairs to shower and get dressed before Omar's stupid ass got to calling and talking shit. That's one impatient ass nigga and I wasn't trying to hear his fuckin mouth today.

I was showered and dressed within thirty minutes, which is good timing for me because I can easily waste a half hour alone in the shower. It's something about that being my place for serenity. Instead of taking the Canary yellow Camaro today, I opted to take my Tahoe instead, since I was on a business move. Black on black big body looks better than a sports car any day when you on a mission. Speeding down I-71 north, I allowed the old skool R&B to beat through my speakers.

You belong to me and only me baby
I belong to you, I belong

I give all my love to you
I give all my love baby

Rome's *I Belong To You* used to be that shit back in the day, and I still jam to this shit when I'm cruising the streets. That's the only thing about me most don't understand. My exterior is rock hard, but when it comes to my music selection, I'll choose R& B any day over Hip Hop. I should've known one of my brothers would be calling me shortly. The moment I turned into the driveway of The Slab, my iPhone started alerting me of a FaceTime call.

"Fuck you want, nigga?" I answered the FaceTime call.

"Fuck you mean what I want? I want your pretty princess ass to hurry the fuck up. I only FaceTimed to make sure your ass wasn't still at the crib taking your precious ass time."

"Nah nigga. I'm outside. I'll be in the in a sec." I said and ended to call so I could head inside.

Walking into my pops' house, I could smell the kush aroma in the air. The crazy thing is, no one ever smoked in my pops' crib, but that's shit was potent. We were expecting a large shipment today and that was the reason for the urgency with my brothers. I headed straight to the basement where we handle all of our business, without even taking a second to chop it up with Bones. Bones had been my pops' head security for years, he was more like family than staff. I would have time to have a few words with him before I left, but at that moment, I needed to get downstairs to see if shit came as expected and if the numbers were adding up.

"Bout got damn time, youngsta. Time waits for no man, except you my friend, huh?" Pops always had some slick shit to say, that's where we got it from.

"What's up, Pops. I had too fucking much to drink last night. I ain't even know it was that late. When Jul called, I thought it was still bout four or five in the morning. Last night was epic, but damn it took a toll on my ass." I said in my defense.

"We see. Nigga was in a deep ass slumber like you on a vacation or something. But enough small talk. The shipment came in about five this morning and after the count and breakdowns, everything is correct. Next thing to do is get it K.R. So we can get it off our hands." Omar said eagerly, ready to be done with our meeting before it really even started.

"Wait, so that nigga K.R. Taking all of the shit? Don't you think that's a bit much for that nigga to handle? Did he have the cash or it's on consignment?" I questioned.

"I don't give two fucks what he can handle. The nigga paid so he gettin all of it, minus maybe two kilos. But he still paying the price of getting five." Omar said with a slight smirk on his face.

"Shit, I don't give a fuck about that nigga. If it wasn't for Jul I would've been cut that nigga off. Something about him don't rub me right." I said while eyeing Jul.

"The nigga ain't never did shit wrong. You can't just go cutting niggas off that's making us money cause you don't like them, but you don't even know why you don't like the nigga. He ain't never did shit wrong to none of us, so until he slips up, we gotta keep him at arm's reach. Shit, the nigga bout his business, I know that much." Jul said with a shrug and headed over to the bar in the corner of the basement. That nigga ain't give a fuck what time of day it was, he was for sure going to drink his 1738.

"Sometimes you have to go off vibes. Never be too trusting of any nigga that bleed the same way you do. Money can cause the most loyal muthafuckas to turn to snakes. If Romeo has a bad vibe about him, y'all better watch him. I don't care how much money he brings in, the money printer ain't stop working when he started getting money." Pops said, and everyone just nodded their head. One thing about Pops, he may not be in the game anymore, but he made it to the age he is now because of the choices he made. Wisdom comes with age and experience, that's for sure one thing I learned from him.

"So what time you doin the drop, Meo?" Mar questioned.

"Shit, soon as we done here. The sooner, the better. Don't we got another shipment coming in about five?" Saturday is our most busy day of the week.

"Yeah, but that shit might be a little late because something happened where the freeway was shut down for a min in his route."

"That's coo. I got a few moves to make between now and then anyway." Jul said as he took another shot of 1738 before heading upstairs. I followed behind him, Mar and Pops followed behind me. As we reached the top of the steps, our movers headed downstairs to pack up the product and get it inside my truck.

Instead of waiting until K.R. called me, I just went to the spot I knew where to find him. I never liked letting niggas know when I would be arriving. Catching people by the element of surprise is how I operated. I always felt like if I warned a nigga of my arrival that would be the easiest way for a muthafucka to think they outsmarting you and set you up or some shit. Not saying half of these niggas was stupid enough to try some shit like that, but you can never be too safe. The Jones name rings bells, and the streets know we ain't shit to play with out here.

"What's up Meo? I wasn't expecting you just yet." K.R. said as he took a puff from his already lit blunt.

"Yeah I know, but it never hurts to be early. When I'm late, that's when it should be a problem." I said with a slight mug on my face.

"Aww nah, it's not a problem, I was just saying." he said while holding his hand up in defense. K.R. gave his nigga a head nod and he exited the area of the room we were in. I threw the two duffle bags on the floor and nodded at him. He knew better than to actually open and count the products in front of me, so he only grinned and continued to smoke his blunt.

"Good looking, Meo. You be safe out here." K.R. Said as I turned to walk out and back to my truck.

"Always!" I said and headed about my way.

POPS TOLD us to postpone our meeting for our evening shipment because he had a gut feeling it was some fuck shit involved, so that meant I was free for the evening. Instead of going to relax at the crib, I decided to stop by the Onyx for happy hour and grab a bite to eat and have a few shots of Patrón to pass time. I could duck off with a bitch, but I'm not in the mood today for some reason.

When I walked into Onyx, I was having second thoughts, because this bitch was jumping like it was a free before nine type of night. Instead of making a U-turn and takin my ass home, I opted to shoot my brothers a text and tell them to join me for happy hour. I knew they would since all of our evenings were freed without our original meeting. Before I could place my phone back in my pocket, I received two message alerts.

Jul: *I'm already here nigga I'm in the back in a VIP section.*

Mar: *I'm headed there now to meet Jul already.*

I shot both of them a text back and headed in the direction of the back of the club. I noticed a few little thots trying to get my attention, but I paid them hoes no mind. They knew money when it walked in the build. Only thing is, I'm not a tricking ass nigga, so their best bet was to keep buying them two for one deals with they EPPICards. You know the card the county gives them for their monthly allowance of sitting at home all damn day on their asses.

When I reached the back where Jul was seated, I noticed he was motioning for the waitress to come over to the table. *Perfect timing!* I thought to myself.

"What's good? Why you ain't tell me you was stopping through here?" I questioned Jul.

"Shit, I thought your ass would be ducked off with some random doing you," he said and started laughing. He had a point, cause if I wasn't getting pesos I was getting pussy, and that's for sure. Those were the only things that I enjoyed doing. Shit, it is what it is. Might as well enjoy this life I was given while I'm here. Every day ain't promised, so while I'm here I'm going to do what makes me happy.

"Shit, normally I would be, but I ain't feeling that shit today. I need a moment to myself, or maybe just something new to catch my attention," I said and we both bust out into laughter.

"Hey, what can I get for you?" A familiar voice caught my attention. I looked up and right into the eyes of Deja. I didn't know she worked here at Onyx. That shit surprised me, because we come here often, and I had never run into her up until now. I couldn't help the slight smile that crept up on my face. From the look on her face, she was happy to see a nigga, too.

"Ummm... Let me get twenty spicy garlic all drums with three cups of bleu cheese. A bottle of 1738 and some cranberry juice, please." Jul gave her his order and she looked over to me.

"And for you?" she asked.

"For starters, how are you today, Miss Deja?"

"I'm doing great today, Mr. Romeo. Thanks for asking." she replied in a polite manner.

"That's good to know. Happy we cross paths again so soon," I gave her a smirk, reminding her of what she promised the next time we crossed paths.

"Well thank you. What can I get you today?" she asked, reminding me she was only over here to take our orders and not to entertain me.

"I'll take ten of your spicy garlic wings all flats with ranch, a side of loaded fries, and a bottle of Patrón, please." I told myself I was only coming here for two shots, but after seeing her face, I wanted to stick around for a little while longer.

"Ok, do you want any chaser for your Patrón?"

"Aww shit yeah, let me get sprite with no ice."

"Ok, I'll be right back with y'all's drinks." she said and walked away from the table.

Even with a pair of bermuda shorts, a tank top and some Air Max '97's Deja was cold. With little effort, she just didn't know how sexy she was. Shawty was applying pressure to these hoes' necks and wasn't even trying hard. She had her hair pulled back to a ponytail with a part down the middle, instead of straight down like she wore it at the party. Her shit was drippy. I could tell it wasn't no bundles or no shit like that, cause of the way her shit was slicked down.

"She was at the party last night, wasn't she?" Jul asked with his face scrunched up like he was trying to remember where he knew her from.

"Yeah, she was with another chick about the same complexion, just a little taller and with a short haircut. I think she said her name was Drea or Dreia, something like that."

"I thought that was her. Dreia caught my attention last night, she gave me her number, but I ain't had the time to hit her up yet, except last night to confirm it was her number."

"Ain't that some shit? I was trying to chop it up with Deja and she straight curved a nigga in a polite way. Almost made me wanna go even harder on her, but Shadeia's ass came from the cut blockin'. I ain't wanna embarrass her ass cause I knew she was drunk, so I just left the shit alone. When I saw her again, she was leaving."

"Ain't that some shit? I always see the waitress Deja, but I only saw the girl Dreia she was with a few time around the city on some humbug shit."

"Shit, I had never seen Deja until last night. That was the first time I ever saw her. I was wondering where she was from cause I'm sure by now I should've been run into her."

"Yeah, I have seen her plenty of times, but I never knew who she was. The most it's ever been between us was her taking my order a couple of times here. Nigga, you've had to saw her at least one time. She been working here for a little minute."

"Nope, never once. I would've been paying attention and been tried to snag her if that was the case."

"Listen to your ass. Pussy always on the brain. Nigga, do you ever think of anything else?" Jul joked.

"Fuck you, nigga." I said as Mar walked up and dapped the both of us up.

"Let me guess, you two fat muthafucka's already placed y'all's order and ain't even think to order my shit," Mar said and took a seat.

As he pulled out his phone and placed it on the table in front of him, Deja walked up with our bottles in her hand, and a chick following behind her with cranberry juice and two cans of Sprite on a tray with a bucket of ice in the other hand.

"I can take your order now. It won't come out long after theirs," Deja said to Mar before either Jul or I could respond. He was right, neither of us thought to order him any food knowing he would be here shortly.

"Thanks, let me get twenty barbeque with a side salad with Italian dressing and a Sweet tea please." Mar ordered his food. I knew Mar wasn't about to drink. That nigga will smoke you to death, but won't take a drink of alcohol for shit.

"Ok, I'll be right back with your drink." Deja said and turned to walk away. I couldn't help but watch the way her hips twisted with every step.

"Nigga, let me find out ol' girl got you mesmerized, youngin." Mar said, and of course, Jul laughed at his corny ass joke.

"Never mesmerized, but shawty cold den a muthafucka and she know it," I said. My phone began to ring, and I looked at it, only to see Shadeia's name appear on my screen. I red buttoned her ass and put her number on the block list. She needed to learn a lesson and what better time than now?

"Yeah, if you say so. Trust me, I see right through that shit you talkin." Mar said and Jul only shook his head.

"Nigga, it ain't nothing to see. I'm speaking facts. No woman has ever had me mesmerized. Honestly, I don't think the shit is possible." I said before placing the bottle of Patrón to my lips, so I could take a nice gulp.

After taking a few drinks of my Patrón, I noticed Deja and the same waitress she had helping her before walking in our direction with trays of food. She wasn't lying when she said that it wouldn't take long. I was expecting to at least have to wait thirty minutes. I'm happy we didn't have to wait because a nigga was starving, but I was prepared if we did have to.

"Here you go, fellas. She's going to bring out some extra napkins and wet wipes. Is there anything else I can get y'all for the moment?" Deja asked as she looked at each of us for our response. When neither of my brothers responded verbally, only shaking their heads, I took that as my cue.

"If you could bring the napkins and wet wipes yourself, I would appreciate it." I said and gave her a devilish grin. Deja rolled her eyes, but she still had a slight smirk on her face, so I knew she was entertained by me.

Just like requested, Deja personally brought back the napkins and wet wipes. When she placed them down on the table, I made an attempt to grab her hand before she was out of arms reach.

"Thank you. If you don't mind, I would like to have your company sometime later today if that's not a problem."

"I don't know if that's possible. I'm actually busy later today." Deja replied.

"Well, how about you shoot me your number and we can work out something for when you are available."

"I'm actually not in the business of what you're looking for, so I'm going to have to politely decline, Mr. Romeo."

I cocked my head to the side slightly because Deja really just curved the shit out of me, but I thought the shit was actually quite flattering.

"And what business might that be?" I needed to know exactly what she thought I was on. I know for damn sure my name rung bells, but in a good way. So why was shawty shooting me down time after time. That hard to get shit only works for so long before either a nigga moves around, or the chick gives in.

"You know exactly what type of business you're in, and I really don't have time to be another number in your phone." Deja said with a smile and walked away before I could even reply.

"Damn, from the sounds of it lil mama ain't got time for no fuck shit with you, Meo." Jul said, and Mar started laughing.

"Nigga I ain't even trying to be on no fuck shit with Shawty. But damn, why she gotta keep shooting a nigga down?" I let out a half of laugh, cause the shit was honestly funny to me.

Deja doesn't know me. No matter what she heard about me, she doesn't personally know me to know what exactly she will be in my phone. It is what it is, and she can think what she wants. But this won't be the end of it, and I guarantee that.

THREE

DREIA

This man has got to be out of his mind if he thinks I'm about to wait around all day for him to drop off my package. Kamar knows I depend on him for my supply, so he uses it to his advantage. I'm a smoker, but I prefer edibles any day over smoking. However, when I don't have a big enough supply to whip something up, I have a guy that will supply me with little quarters here and there at no charge because he likes me. Deuce and I met a couple of months ago, when Kamar and I first broke up, at the car wash. The only reason I exchanged numbers with him was because Deja's nosey ass was in the car and yelled off my number to him when he requested it. Deja is always trying to play the big sister role and run somebody's damn life. She has nothing but good intentions, so I never fuss at her, but I wasn't ready, and I'm still not honestly, ready to move on.

Other than Kamar being what I would like to refer to as my business partner, he was also my lover. Kamar and I have been dealing with each other for almost three years on and off. Before we made it official, we were friends, so we have a nice amount of history that always encourages me to go back to him because he is what I know and what I'm comfortable with. It wasn't until a couple of months that I decided to break up and leave Kamar for good. That's when Deja and I decided to move in together.

Kamar and I are at two different places in life. He still finds enjoyment out of fucking and dealing with multiple women at once, and I'm ready to settle down. I've been ready to settle down and be with one person, I thought he was too, three years ago. But after the first year, I discovered he wasn't. The first time I caught Kamar cheating hurt the worst. Every time I found out something after that, it's almost like I expected it. The question is, if I expected it and become accustomed to it, why would I allow it to continue for so long? My answer to myself was always because I loved him, and I knew he was capable of being the man I needed him to be. The problem is the same man I know he is capable of being and see in him, he doesn't see in himself, or he would be working towards becoming that man instead of getting worse as time goes on.

The longer I stayed with him, the worse it got. It went from cheating once to cheating over and over with multiple women. It got to the point where I stopped asking about the shit. Maris always told us growing up if you don't plan on leaving a man for what you're confronting him about, there's no purpose to confront him. She told us when a man discovers you're allowing of bullshit behaviors, he'll keep going and keep trying you until you take action. So, without action, there should be no confrontation about it. I made the mistake of confronting him the first time and forgiving him without any consequences, and just as she warned it got worse gradually, to the point I began to feel like I was losing myself by being with him.

We separated, but I continued to have sex with him because I'm not ready to give myself to someone new yet, or should I say, I haven't taken the time to meet anyone new worth giving myself to. I also get my weed from him for my edibles. I own and operate a small business where I make several different types of edibles. Kamar is my supplier, and until I find someone else I can trust to get me product that is of good quality and a decent price, I have to continue to go through him. We both benefit from it, so right now I'm just going with the flow.

It's hard loving a person and not being able to be with them when you thought they were your forever. But before I sit back and play the role of a weak woman or his footstool, I'll be alone until that time is right. I love him and will always love him, but that doesn't mean I have to be with him. Kamar knows the place he holds in my heart and that's the reason he does the shit he does.

Just as I was about to text him for the third time to check his whereabouts, I heard a knock on the front door. Eagerly racing to open the door, I damn near tripped over the bags on the floor. I went out earlier today and restocked on all my supplies, and instead of putting them up while waiting on Kamar, I simply sat on the kitchen counter scrolling through my phone and online shopping. Another bad habit of mine.

"Hey!" I greeted Kamar as I welcomed him in.

"What's up with you today?" Kamar asked as he reached for my waist with his free arm and placed a slight peck on the nape of my neck.

"Nothing much, waiting on your slow tail so I can start. I have fifteen orders to ship out and I have six orders that are locals I need to get done within the next few hours."

"Ok ok, sounds like you got a busy day. What're your plans once you finished?" Kamar asked. I'm sure he probably wanted some, but I had no intentions of giving him any ass today.

"By the time I'm finished I'll be tired as hell I'm sure. I have been ripping and running all day already."

"You got time for me tonight? I was thinking maybe we could get a room or do something."

Kamar was trying it, cause he knew damn well he wasn't trying to do anything other than bust a nut. Now don't get me wrong, I did say I still fuck with him, but it's on my terms. If I gave Kamar some ass whenever he wanted, he would have the upper hand, and I'm over that stage with him. So, when we have sex now, it's on my terms and my terms only. I can't pretend like I don't have weak moments here and there, but they aren't half as frequent as they were at the beginning of our split.

"I may, I'll let you know once I'm done with everything for the day." I partially lied, because I knew I wasn't meeting up with Kamar tonight. I would, however, send him a text just seeing what he's doing and make sure he's ok. Kamar lives a risky life, so that's the least I could do.

"Bet. Well here's your goods, I threw in a little extra for you. It's about a pound and half or a little less."

"Thanks, do I owe you anything more?"

"Nah you coo, it's on me. That should last you until next week, right?" Kamar asked.

"I appreciate it. Yeah, this should last me unless I get slammed in orders." I said as I grabbed the bag he was carrying my product in and carried it away to the kitchen to start my cooking process.

"I'mma let you get back to what you're doing, and I'll hit you up a little later." Kamar said as he walked up behind me and wrapped his arms around me to say his goodbye.

"You be careful." I said to him as I turned to grab my favorite pot to cook in.

"I will." Kamar headed out and I followed behind to lock the front door.

IT TOOK me a little longer than expected to complete the orders, but I was happy when I finally completed them. The online orders that I needed to complete were all for chocolate chip cookies. After baking up ten dozen cookies, the bulk of my work was completed. All of the local orders were for pound cakes and banana bread, so that didn't take too long. Using muffin pans helped me to get done a lot quicker. I called up Destini to pick up the two orders she placed for people, and the other four were for people at Deja's job.

"Damn, I don't know if I'm going to pass out from contact of the aromas or start eating all these damn goodies cause of the smell. The mixture between baked goods and weed is powerful as fuck." Destini said as she walked through the front door. Destini had a key to our place just like we each had one to hers. My sisters and I have always been very close, and no matter whether we all live under the same roof or not, things remain the same.

"It doesn't bother me. I think I'm immune to it at this point. I don't even eat anything while I'm cooking it. I remember when I first started, I would snack while cooking and by the time I was done, I would need to create another batch of whatever it was because of the munchies I would eat so much."

"I would never be able to get immune to this shit. I don't know how y'all eat them thangs. After that one time I ate a piece of yours, I've never touched another. I don't like how being high makes me feel. I'll stick to my drinks. Now that's what you need to be working on next. Making goodies with alcohol. I'm not talking about infused with the little dropper, either. I'm talking about cooked from scratch like you do these treats." Destini had never been a smoker, and no matter how many times Deja and I tried to make her one, she just couldn't handle it.

"I thought about it but, you know I'm not big on drinks, so I've been putting it off. But I promise you I will try it soon in the future, and you'll have to be the one who samples them and let me know the quality of them."

"I'm all for that, just make sure the first thing you try is cheese-cake. I think a Patrón or 1800 cheesecake would be so bomb. Oh my goodness, I can taste that shit now."

"Listen to you! Mouth over there watering already. I'll work on it soon, I promise."

"Girl, you know how I feel about cheesecake and you know how I feel about my liquor. Can't go wrong with having both of them in one." Destini joked. "Alright, let me get out of here. I got a few things I got to take care of for the Center after I drop this order off. Here's your money too, before I forget." Destini handed me the money and I gratefully took it fast as hell.

"Oh, don't worry, I wasn't going to let you forget. You and Dej are the only people who don't pay in advance, so I need all my coins upon pickup." I joked.

"I know that's right. Better make that money, honey!" We both started laughing because I had really turned a hobby and pastime into a small business that was making great profit at this point. I'm only about six months in and I have already touched over twenty thousand dollars off of my edibles alone. I quit my job at the college as a lead cook and started baking, just on the strength I hated clocking in and being told when and what to do. I didn't think that I would make so much so fast, but I'm thankful I finally took a leap of faith and tried it.

Like I knew I would, I ended up lounging around in my room watching random shows on Netflix instead of trying to meet up with Kamar. I did shoot him a text and let him know I was in for the night and we could link up maybe tomorrow. He didn't reply, so my guess is he was busy anyway, go figure. The thing about Kamar is, I knew him far better than he knew me, and I knew if I didn't give him some ass like he wanted he would go elsewhere. Only thing is, he didn't know at this point I don't even care. Well, at least I'm training myself not to care anymore.

My phone chimed a couple of times and I ignored it because I was so into the damn movie, until I paused for a second to go grab me a glass of lemonade from the kitchen. Walking downstairs, I scrolled through my phone to see who had texted me and to my surprise, it was the guy Julian from the all-white party. I had totally forgotten I gave him my number. A part of me wanted to ignore his message, but I decided not to and sent a short reply.

One text turned into a night full of texting. Before I knew it, it was damn near two o'clock in the morning and he was calling my phone. I didn't want to answer because it was a FaceTime call, but since I had nothing to lose, I thought why not.

"Hey, what made you FaceTime me?" I questioned the moment our call was connected.

"I just wanted to see your beautiful face and to make sure you wasn't laid up texting me." Julian joked. I knew there was some truth to what he said, cause had it not been, he would've continued to text instead.

"You're silly. I told you it's just me and my sister that live together. No funny business going on over here. Secondly, I would never be disrespectful enough to text you for hours on end if I was laid up. Not only would that be disrespectful toward you, but to the person I'm laid up with as well."

I needed him to know out the gate I wasn't that type of chick. If I'm with a person, that's who I'm with, and I don't have time to entertain the next when I could be using that energy to keep the one I'm with happy.

"I hear you, but the mouth can say a million things and the body does otherwise." Julian said before taking a puff from his lit blunt. I could tell by his background that he had to be lying in bed also. I wondered what a man like himself would be up late night alone as well.

"I see you're in the bed, too. I'm normally not up this late, but our conversation was flowing pretty good, so my attention was well kept." I informed him.

"Same here. Well, I'm always up late, but our conversation definitely had all my attention. I expected you to have a head wrap or something on and hiding your face, but I'm glad you didn't. I mean, either way I wouldn't mind, but I'm just saying." I couldn't hold in my laughter because he was right about the head wrap things, considering it was late night.

"Nah, not tonight. I have a hair appointment tomorrow so there's really no need for me to wrap my hair up. How about yourself, what's your plans for tomorrow?" I questioned. Julian was sexy as hell and looking at him for too long would be all bad. I ate a few too many edibles while watching movies, and texting him over the last few hours had my cat throbbing for some attention.

"My schedule is free tomorrow. I would like to take you out to lunch or something if that's ok with you." It had been so long since I'd been on an actual date I didn't know whether to decline or to take him up on his offer.

"Yeah, that's fine. Around what time were you thinking of meeting up?"

"Whatever time works for you? I'll be free, but we aren't meeting up. I want to take you out, so I'll be picking you up. I don't have to come to your home if you're not comfortable with that. I can pick you up from the hair salon when you're done with that. Whatever works best for you is what we're going to do." The way he was making the whole date idea about me was very thoughtful, but that's exactly how all men start out in the beginning, until they get you right where they want you.

"My hair appointment is at noon, so I should be done no later than one. You can pick me up from there."

He was right, I didn't want him knowing where I stayed at just yet. I'm sure him being a Jones brother, he could find out if he really wanted to because them niggas got power and connections all over. But we are only friends and I just met him, so I for damn sure wasn't going to tell him where I lived.

"That's fine, what salon do you go to?"

"Oohs and Ahs by Eastland Mall."

"That's crazy, I go there for my lineups. Well I go to the barbershop a couple doors down by the same name." How ironic was that he got his hair cut by the same company that I go get my hair done. Let's hope like hell him picking me up from the shop doesn't draw too much attention from other customers or workers in the shop. I'd hate to have people speculating and all in my business. Kamar knows too many people and Julian Jones is a well-known man. Deja told me all about him after that night when we got home. She was drunk, so she kept yapping and yapping about them Jones brothers and what she knew about them. She talked herself to sleep about them Jones brothers. If I didn't know any better, I would think she had done a research paper on the three men.

"Wow, I'm surprised I haven't ran into you at the shops before."

"I'm normally in and out pretty early before they actually open."

"That makes perfect sense. Look at you, presidential services." I joked.

"Nah, I just don't have time to be waiting on my barber to finish up folks. Time is money and I don't like wasting it."

"I totally can understand that. I'm bout to get off this phone and call it a night before I wake up super late dealing with you." I said in closing of our conversation because I felt my eyes getting lower and lower. No matter how much I wanted to be into the conversation and continue talking with Julian, I was already tired and too high to fight my sleep any longer.

"Yeah, go ahead and get you some rest. I'll talk with you tomorrow, sweety." Julian said.

"Talk to you tomorrow, good night." I said, and we ended our call. Before I could get my phone completely on the charger, my eyes were closing.

I EXPECTED to sleep in later than I did because I stayed up talking to Julian, but Deja had other plans for my rest, obviously. She cooked breakfast and brought it to me in bed, then convinced me to get up and go shopping with her before my hair appointment. Anyone who knows me knows shopping is my thing, so it's hard for me to resist.

Instead of driving my car, I just rode with Deja and opted to have her drop me off at the shop once we were finished shopping. I actually did rather good by not overspending. I grabbed myself a few cute little sandals, two outfits, and some little accessories. I was paranoid about the outfit I was wearing, because I didn't know what type of place Julian had in mind to take me. So I decided to wear one of the outfits I purchased out of the store. Dej told me that it was an all-purpose outfit so I that helped to ease my mind some. I felt like a one-piece catsuit with a jean jacket was a bit much, but if Dej thought it looked fine, I guess I'm coo. I walked into the salon at exactly noon. Shea already finished with her client prior to me, so I sat right in the chair. No matter how many clients she books, Shea always gets you straight in and straight out. The quality of her work is still just as great with every appointment, which is the reason me and my sisters continued to come back to her year after year. We've been rocking with her before she even became a licensed stylist, and that's how it's going to remain.

Julian sent me a text letting me know he would be outside waiting for me when I got done five minutes till one. Since I was just getting done, I went to the restroom to look myself over and make sure that I was presentable. After paying Shea, I headed out to meet my date. I wasn't sure what car he was in, so I was happy to see him standing outside of the passenger door, holding it open for me. He must've been watching from the outside of the shop, because he was on point with his timing.

"Hello, beautiful!" Julian greeted me.

"Hey, how are you?" I greeted him in return.

"I'm alright. How about yourself?"

"I'm doing well. Thank you." I said as I slid into the passenger side of his all-white Chevy Corvette. I wasn't sure of the year, but I could tell from the new smelling interior it couldn't be that old. Julian walked around to the driver's side of the car and hopped right in.

"So, is there anywhere, in particular, you are against going to?" Julian questioned.

"No, I'm open to wherever you wanna go. I'm not a very picky eater, so no matter where we go, I'm sure I can find something I like on the menu." I honestly told him.

"So, since it's still lunchtime we can go by one of my favorite places. I hope you'll enjoy it as much as I do."

"And where might that be?" I asked.

"It's called Mitchell's Ocean Club in Easton. You ever ate there?"

"Umm, I think I went one time before with my sisters, but I only had appetizers. We only stopped by to have a drink since we were out browsing through Easton one day."

"Oh coo. Their drinks are good, but their food is even better." Julian assured me.

When we arrived at Easton, Julian had valet park the car and walked around to assist me getting out. I was pleased by the kind gestures and the way he was so well-mannered. For him to be such a big deal and so popular, I honestly thought he wouldn't be so humble, but yet instead very arrogant, which he wasn't. Walking through Easton, I noticed a couple of females eyeing us, but I didn't think anything of it because I knew what type of man I was going on a date with when I agreed to it. Then when Julian reached to hold my hand while we were walking, let me know he didn't mind the looks and stares either. It made me kind of shy and nervous at first, I can't lie. I was more than anxious to get inside of the restaurant, so I could order a drink to take my nerves off edge a bit.

The hostess knew Julian by name. The moment we walked up, he was greeted by his last name. Then the fact that he had a special section that he preferred to sit in let me know just how much of a regular he really was. The moment we were seated, they immediately were ready to take our orders. Julian ordered a drink called Old Fashioned for himself, and I stuck to the drink I had the last time I came here, which was the Club Margarita. I took a second to look over the menu while Julian ordered himself Surf and Turf. I had no clue what it was until I read the description on the menu. An 8-ounce filet, buttered poached lobster Gouda potato cake, Chili seared spinach, Cabernet truffle reduction and béarnaise seemed like a lot to eat, but Julian isn't a small guy, so I believe he can eat all that food. Julian stands at least six-foot-three. I'm going guess and say he weighs about

280 pounds, and he's very stocky build. His long dreads and goatee compliment him well. Normally I'm not into the lighter-skinned guys, but something about his golden-brown skin complexion is very enticing. Finally, I discovered what I wanted on the menu. I ordered Twin Lobster tails with asparagus and drawn butter.

While waiting for our food to come, we held small talk about ourselves. I was shocked to find out that Julian was thirty years old without any children, he's never been married, and only had one serious relationship in his life. For a man to make it to thirty with no children and no wife is rare. Especially when they have as much to offer as Julian. Julian explained to me that he's a businessman from both aspects of life. I didn't ask the details when he said both sides of life, because I already knew what he was referring to other than the corporate businesses he partakes in. I'm glad he was honest, but I still didn't want to know much about it. Julian told me that he just recently started his own construction company, and that it was actually doing pretty good. He doesn't do any of the actual work himself, he just owns and operates it. I found that to be very exciting because you hear about people starting all types of companies, but never their own construction firm. It takes a lot of money and connections to do such, and that he has.

Since he was so open and honest with me, I decided to do the same with him. I explained that I had been in a long-term relationship that just ended recently and I'm still in communication with him, but we have nothing serious between us anymore. I didn't tell him Kamar's name because I didn't feel that it was of any importance. He didn't ask, so I didn't tell. Rule of thumb, if it doesn't affect you two, it shouldn't be discussed. Especially considering I was just getting to know Julian.

After we ate and had several drinks while talking, we finally left the restaurant. I hadn't realized we were sitting and enjoying each other's company for so long that it was almost 5 o'clock by the time we got out of there. Julian asked did I want to stop by any stores while we were walking around Easton, and I kindly declined. Little did he know, shopping is my weakness and him treating me to a nice yet very expensive meal, I figured he had done enough. Besides, I was feeling the drinks we had over our conversation. I hoped like hell I wasn't slurring. I'm not a big drinker, so I was buzzed after the first two drinks. However, being under the influence of alcohol allowed me to be more free and comfortable with him.

FOUR

JULIAN

The sight of her neatly waxed pussy had my mind blown. I had yet to see a pussy so pretty in my life, but something about her made me want to sit and stare for hours instead of devouring it like I planned on. Wrapping my arms around her thighs, I pulled her closer to my face and used my tongue to softly lick around her opening. I used my tongue to part her lips and began to flicker it across her clit. Her pussy smelled fresh as if she had just taken a shower, and we had been out kicking it all day. The taste had a hint of strawberry, and I thought I was tripping for a minute, but I wasn't.

Dreia gently grabbed my head and began to grind her hips into my face harder and harder. Just feeling her getting into it only motivated me to please her even more, using my tongue to take Dreia to different heights she had yet to ever reach, and I knew this by her reactions. I had already made her cum prematurely, but I could tell she was about to reach a massive orgasm by the way her body stiffened up and her moans became seductive screams. I was enjoying pleasing her far more than I have ever before. Normally, I'm not the type to just go down on a woman, and especially not the first night. But something about Dreia, I had to taste her.

Once she reached her climax, I slowly eased off her clit because I knew it was sensitive as fuck from all the pleasure I had just given her. I sat up and reached into my nightstand dresser drawer to retrieve a condom and began to open the package. I knew if she tasted that good she felt even better, but I wasn't about to just slide inside of her without any protection. She's not my woman, and I'd hate to get into the heat of the moment and let loose all inside of her. We aren't an item yet, but after today we for damn sure ain't about to be just friends either.

Sliding the condom down my dick, I watched as she eyed me seductively and licked her lips. I couldn't tell if she was just pleased with the package I was working with, or if she wanted to taste me, but I wasn't going to pressure her either way. It's not like I needed any of her assistance getting my shit hard because tasting her had already done that for me. Dreia crawled over to me and gently climbed on top. Slowly sliding down my dick, I felt her walls adjusting and pulsating as I was entering her. My dick fit her pussy like a glove and her juices were flowing heavily. I didn't think she would have much left in her after the tongue lashing, but she did.

She wasted no time getting comfortable and beginning to wind her hips on top of me. Instead of Dreia positioning herself on her feet flat, she was on her knees riding me like a pro. Winding her hips and bouncing at a rapid pace, I had to control myself. I began to fuck her back from the bottom, while biting down on my bottom lip. Hearing her fat ass smack my thighs as she bounced only turned me on even more. Dreia had a thing about making eye contact while having sex, I didn't mind looking into her eyes because she was mesmerizing. From the way her eyes rolled in the back of her head to the sexy ass moans that escaped her lips, I couldn't even concentrate enough to do anything besides squeezing her ass firmly.

Unlike most women, Dreia didn't announce when she was about to reach her climax. Had I not been able to tell the difference in the way her pussy was reacting, I would never know because her pussy juices were overflowing even without her cumming. Shortly after she reached her last climax, I felt my nut building and I wrapped my arms around her and took control. Laying her on her back and pushing her legs back by her ankles, seeing how comfortable she was in the position gave me the ok to beat her shit up. I increased the pace and started giving her deep, long strokes. I thought she was done, but she began to squirt uncontrollably, causing me to nut simultaneously with her before I was even prepared to.

Hearing Dreia's phone continuously go off woke me out my sleep. I'm surprised she didn't hear it, because it was right next to her on the nightstand. Instead, she continued to enjoy her deep slumber. I put her in a coma-like state with the session we had earlier. Our plan was never to fuck and lay-up, but that's what happened. All the drinking took over us, I couldn't control my actions, and neither could she.

"Beautiful, wake up." I said as I gently shook Dreia, so she could answer her phone.

"Oh, my goodness. What time is it?" She jumped up as if she was about to be tardy for work or some shit.

"It's almost three in the morning. Your phone kept ringing and I thought you might want to answer it because they keep callin back." I know when my phone continuously goes off it's something important, so I thought the same for her. She reached over and looked at her phone and placed it back on the nightstand after pressing a few buttons.

"My sister isn't used to me staying away from home. She wanted to make sure that I was ok."

"You straight? You wanna go home?" I questioned because I wasn't for keeping anyone against their own will. I enjoyed her company, and I for damn sure liked the sex, but I ain't forcing shit.

"Yeah, I'm fine. It's too late to have you drive me across town to my place."

It was pretty late, but I'm used to being up late, so it didn't bother me. Had I not had all those drinks with her and fucked the way we did, I probably would've still been up. We were only supposed to stop by my house, so I could change. But we ended up staying here and talking, which led to sex. The lunch date turned into to an all-day event full of surprises.

Dreia snuggled up against me and I wrapped my arm around her small frame. Just like that, we were both fast asleep as if it had never been interrupted.

"Good Morning, beautiful." I greeted Dreia as I walked into the room and she was just opening her eyes.

"Good morning. How long have you been awake?" she asked as she wiped the sleep from her eyes.

"I got up around eight thirty. I'm a morning person, I can't sleep in past a certain hour, no matter how late I stay up the night before. I was going to cook you something to eat for breakfast, but then I remembered I don't know what you like and don't like so I decided not to."

"Aww, how thoughtful. I'm not really an eater. As soon as I wake up, I have to get my day started then eat, but I appreciate the thought."

"Well good thing I didn't cook, I would've wasted my culinary skills for nothin."

"I would've nibbled a little just so you wouldn't feel some type of way, but that's it." she said as she retrieved her phone and began to reply to missed messages and calls. For her to be single, her phone went off a lot. If I didn't know any better, I would think her ex-nigga still had close tabs on her. Ain't no way in hell her sister blowing her up that much. I'm not going speak on it just yet, but when the time is right I will.

"As bad as I would love to cuddle up under you all day, I have to get showered and myself together. Do you mind if I call an Uber to take me home, or is your location something you don't care to share?" she asked.

"I know my crib may seem far out and ducked off, but trust me I'm not worried about anyone knowing my location. Moved away from the inner city for the peace of mind, not to hide. You don't have to call an Uber. What type of man would I be to allow you to take an Uber home? I don't mind driving you, that's if you don't mind me knowing where you stay."

"Oh, that's no biggie. I mean, I know where you stay, and after last night it's a little bit too late to try to be secretive with you. I've already shared my most prized possession with you."

"I was thinking that, but I wanted to make sure. Go ahead and get your stuff together and I'll be downstairs waiting for you when you're ready." I said and headed downstairs to my living room. Unlike Dreia, I was a morning eater and a nigga was starving. Quiet as kept, I was ready for her ass to wake up, so I could go grab me a deluxe breakfast sandwich from somewhere. Waking up at eight thirty, and it's damn near noon, my stomach is almost touching my back already.

I noticed while taking Dreia home, she was really quiet. My assumption was she had to be in deep thought. I tried to spark a little conversation with her, but she was really short, not in a smart-alecky type of way, but just as if she had a lot on her mind at the moment. When we got to her place, I was happy to see that she was living in a decent area in a nice condo. Like always, I stepped out of the car to open her door and walk her to the doorstep. That's when Deja opened the door for us, giving a goofy grin. It's almost like she was surprised to see her with me. I'm sure they would discuss how last night went, because that's what ladies do. I'm not worried about her discussing me to anyone, because whatever I do comes with no shame.

We said our goodbyes and she promised to hit me up after she got some work done. I know she told me that she baked for a living, but I was curious to know how she was baking and I never heard about her. I try to support all local businesses, but I had never heard of her. "Elevated Desserts" is the name of her company, and since I had yet to support or try any of her product, I made a mental note to make a large contribution to her company in the near future.

"YOU MEAN to tell me they can't get sixteen kilos across I-35? How hard can that fucking be? We've had double that amount sent several times, yet he's the only driver that's unable to get shit done." My pops was on his business phone going off about a shipment of coke we were supposed to have last weekend but had yet to receive.

Instead of adding my two cents, I patiently waited for him to end the call while I sipped my 1738. The shit was starting to irritate my soul. That's one million six hundred thousand street value that these people playing with, and I need all my ends. One thing I don't like is for a muthafucka to play when it comes to my line of business. My brothers and I had already made the decision to make the trip our damn selves. It's our product and it's our time, so why not take care of it our damn selves. That's the difference in a lot of muthafuckas. We live this life, they just speak on it.

"That was the last run for his career. I don't trust his movement and I don't have time to play about my money." My pops said and ended the call.

"Rambo was the only nigga I trusted from the gate. I don't know why we even tried to allow this silly looking ass dude to take on something like that." Meo complained.

"Yeah, but with Rambo out the country, I was told he would be the next best thing. I see now that he isn't. I'm glad it was a light load we were copping, because had it been our normal thirty-two kilos, I would've been on the jet headed there now."

"Well, this what we gone do, we going to catch a flight down there purchase a truck and drive the shit back our damn selves. That way, ain't no room for error or mistakes if we got our own shit." Meo was the most impatient of us all, so I expected him to be ready to hit the road the moment Pops hung up the line.

"That's fine but make sure you handle him while y'all down there. This is something I never want to experience again. It makes the business too hot. He's driving a fucking eighteen wheeler doing circles going back and forth like that's not obvious or on their radar."

Pops already knew how we were coming, so honestly, it wasn't any need to tell us to handle him. It didn't make any sense for us not to. He knew too much information for us to flat out fire him. He had one job and couldn't get that done.

We sat around for about thirty minutes or so chopping it up with my pops before heading to the spot where we would take the jet to Texas and get our products. It was an unexpected trip we would have to make, but when it comes to our Cartel, there's no time to play. I sent Dreia a text letting her know something came up and I needed to take a trip, but I would be in contact with her while I was gone. I just wouldn't see her for a few days. She didn't reply back right away, so I figured she was busy. The ride back from Texas wouldn't be too bad because we would take turns driving until we make it back. But it's still damn near seventeen hours. Pops never ships large amounts of product in the air, so driving was the only option. The pilot would just return after dropping us off.

After boarding the jet, I lit my blunt and reclined my seat. It's only an hour ride but I'mma need this hour to relax my mind and calculate my next move. Mar's ass had his head in his phone from the moment we left The Slab. Meo, on the other hand, was silent. Normally when he gets silent, it's because he's on some bullshit. He's not much of a talker when it's time for action, so I already knew how shit was about to play out once we landed in Texas.

I hadn't even realized that I dozed off until Meo woke me up saying that we had landed. I grabbed my phone from my lap and proceeded to exit the jet. RJ was waiting for us to take us to purchase a new truck. Shit, the truck would be used primarily for shit like this, so it was well needed anyways. I mean, we all have multiple cars each, but this would just be considered to be a business vehicle. RJ is Rambo's son, and although he doesn't do the drops, he's about his business with everything else. I'm sure RJ already knew if he was seeing the Jones brothers unexpectedly like this, there were going to be consequences for this nigga Ron. Ron had to be new in the game for him to be making bad blood so soon, or he just didn't value his life. Either way, it's over with now.

RJ drove us to a car lot that he and his father did business with often. They had four different big body SUVs lined up, waiting for us to choose from. RJ already knew the style of truck we were interested in before we landed, so he must've made that call to have things in line for our arrival. It was a tough decision because we all were fans of the Chevy family, but that Benz truck was looking nice as fuck. I made plans to contact the dealership as soon as I got back to the city, so I could grab one of those for my personal use.

RJ gave us the information on where to meet up with Ron, who thought RJ was meeting him to get the merchandise. But he was in for a rude awakening. The moment we got to the vacant lot used for Semi-truck drivers, Meo started to hand us guns. You never know what to expect when dealing with people. Just in case Ron was on some funny shit with RJ, we were prepared. Ron must've noticed the black Avalanche heading his way, because he was hopping out of the Semi as we were parking. He headed straight for the rear of the Semi, preparing to unload. The was the wrong move already. You never open the cargo until the people you are meeting up with are next to you. That's the easiest way for some shit to get set off.

Meo did make sure the truck was in park before he hopped out and headed in the direction of Ron. Mar was right on his trail. I left the truck running because it wouldn't take long to load it and be on our way back to Ohio. Mar didn't say a word to Ron, instead Meo took him to the side and started talking to him while Mar and I unloaded the merchandise and loaded up the different stash spots of our truck.

"It all makes sense now why the nigga was taking his time with getting our shit to us. I can tell just by the packages that it's short," Mar said to me as he headed in the direction of Meo and Ron. I kept my eyes open for any bystanders while taking my burner phone out to call RJ and let him know to send in the crew to pick up the Semi and clean up the mess Meo and Mar were about to make.

As I ended the call, I heard the silencer begin to go off. That was my cue to head to the truck. As I walked over to the truck I took a look back and noticed Ron slumped on the pavement, bleeding out. I shook my head and hopped in to wait for them two. The nigga got what was coming to him. You never play with a man's money, especially men like the Jones brothers. With power like ours, we could've had him taken care of easily without a second thought. But that's what made our name hold so much weight, we handle our own dirty work. We handle things the first time a mistake is made, never allowing anything to slide. If you give a person a free pass one time, they try again and think you're ok with whatever they did.

By the time Meo and Mar got to the truck, RJ and his men were pulling up. I rolled the driver's side window down and gave him a head nod. He did the same and we were headed on our way home. My phone chimed, and I noticed Dreia's name appear on the screen. It gave a nigga a good feeling inside, although I was a little curious as to why I was just hearing back from her. I last texted her early this morning when we decided to take this trip. It's damn near midnight and I'm just getting a response.

Dreia: *Hey sweetie I had a busy day with orders. Sorry, I'm just getting back to you. Did you make it to your destination yet?*

Me: *Hey beautiful. It's no problem. Yeah, I'm headed back home now.*

Dreia: *So soon. I thought you were going to be gone a couple of days?*

Me: *Yeah, I'm done so my visit was cut short. Is that a problem that I'm coming back so soon?*

Dreia: *No not at all. Why would it be?*

Me: *I'm just asking. I need a taste of Dreia anyways so the moment I get back in the city I hope you're free.*

Dreia: *A taste of me huh? Is that right? So soon?*

Me: *What you mean so soon. Shit, it's been a couple of days. Ima nympho baby if I get a taste of something I like I need it daily multiple times a day.*

Dreia: *Oh ok.*

Me: *Is that going to be a problem?*

Dreia: *No not at all. I'll be ready for you when you get back.*

Me: *That's what I like to hear. I'm driving though baby, so I'll be getting with you as soon as I get to the city.*

Dreia: *Ok drive safe. Talk to you later.*

I could taste Dreia's pussy on my lips already. That shit only made me increase my speed a little, which I could tell put Mar on edge because he said something about me slowing down some. I wasn't stupid, I wasn't about to drive recklessly and get us pulled over, but I wasn't trying to drive the entire trip doing the speed limit. When it was his turn to drive, he could do sixty-five the whole way home. But as long as I'm behind the wheel, I'm gone drive what I feel.

FIVE
DESTINI

Between working and my personal life, I swear I'm about to drive myself crazy. The youth center that I own and operate is growing at a rapid rate, and I'm starting to think I'm in over my head. I wanna hire more staff, but I don't just want to hire any ol' person off the streets. I sometimes wish that my sisters were as active and into children like I am, cause I know for a fact they wouldn't let me down. But all we're in different fields of occupation. On a brighter note, I have Maris helping me, because she adores children of all ages. Had it not been for her, I don't think I would be able to keep pushing when it comes to this business.

Maris got custody of my sisters and I when I was only seven, Dreia was three and Deja was only a couple of weeks old. She's been the mother we never had for as long as I can remember. Our real mother, I don't know, and could care less to know anything about. The only things I remember from childhood was being passed from foster home to foster home, being molested and ending up with Miss Maris. After Miss Maris got custody of us, our lives took a turn for the better. We were no longer bouncing from home to home, and she always treated us as if we were her birth children. She told us she wasn't able to be the mother she desired to be, so this was her second chance. We never questioned her, because she said it was in the past and wanted to leave it there, so that's where we left it.

Because of the things I experienced as a child is why I wanted to help youth now that I'm grown and established. The youth center is a twenty-four-hour safe house that offers a variety of things for all ages. We offer daycare-like programs, safe house, clothing, day camps, and activities. Everything's funded by grants I received or my own personal savings. Originally, I wanted to make it a non-profit, but I went in a different direction shortly after opening it. The center has been up and running now for almost three years, and it's expanding now that everything is in place and people are hearing about the great things that take place at the center.

I tried to make Miss Maris co-owner, but she declined, telling me she would play the role but without any title. She explained that that's what she was here for, and that she would help out in any aspect without pay or titles. I appreciated Miss Maris more than she would ever know. Because of her, my sisters and me are who we are today. I know it sounds funny for me to call the only mother figure I have in my life by her first name, but that's how she brought us up. She felt like it was disrespect to call another woman mom who didn't give birth to you, no matter the circumstances. I totally disagreed with her, but after being corrected so many times, we just continued to call her Miss Maris.

Today, I had a meeting with a few city councilmen about some grants I had applied for, to get transportation for children in different parts of the city, to have access to the center if they weren't able to be transported by their parents. Everything went well, but I needed to get a few more things together on my end before everything could be finalized. I would've been taken care of it had I not been sidetracked by Omar's ass. That man got my nose wide the fuck open, and I can't even blame him for my laziness, no matter how hard I wanted to.

Yes, Omar Jones is my little secret. We have been dealing with each other for quite some time, but no one knows. I'm a very private person because of the role I play in my community, and the life Omar lives can either be great or detrimental to my success. I know he has a lot of control and pull, but one wrong move and all the good things about him can turn to shit. If he and his family were to ever get in legal troubles they can't get out of, you better believe they will be under the jail without ever seeing the light of day.

Dealing with Omar on a personal level for so long, I've learned all the ropes to his lifestyle. I love the fact that he's a man about his money, but I hate the fact that jail or death are his only two ways out of it. Omar and I are only friends, but lately, I've been thinking of taking it to the next level with him. I mean, after a year of dealing with him and only him it's only right. The only reason I've waited this long to make anything official with him is because that man has hella groupies and I ain't got time to catch a case cause a bitch has to catch this fade.

Omar would be the perfect man if he could control the number of women he deals with. It's not half as bad as when I first met him, but I'm not stupid either. The only reason I know he ain't only dealing with me at this point is because his phone goes off too much after hours for it to be business only. I'm no dummy, but since he's technically not my man, it's only so much I really can complain about. He plays the role of my man in many ways, but he's not. Omar is there for me physically, sexually, and financially, but that title just doesn't exist as of right now. I think this is something I'm going to discuss with him later this week, because I'm getting too old to be playing this shacking up game with anyone.

Just as I was sending out the last email before I headed home for the day, my phone rang and it was Omar.

"Hey, Zaddy!" I greeted Omar.

"Hey, baby. You almost done at the office? I need a daily dose of my Tini." I felt my pussy jump when he said that shit.

"Zamn Zaddy yess. Where you at?"

"Bout to head to your crib to meet you if you're almost done."

"Ok coo, I'll meet you there give me like twenty minute." I said and ended our call.

I walked out and told Miss Maris I was done for the day and I would call her this evening. I practically ran to the fucking car. My pussy was doing the moving for me. We just fucked all night, but that didn't change the fact when he calls and even mentions it, I'm ready to get it in some more. I don't think I could ever get enough of that dope dick. It's like a fucking Pringle, once I popped I couldn't stop.

Omar was pulling up to my condo the moment I pulled into my garage. I waited until he pulled his car inside too before I closed the garage door. The moment both of our feet were in the door, Omar was all over me. Damn near ripping my form fitting dress off of me. When he pushed me over the back of the sofa, so I was face down in the pillow with my ass up, I prepared myself for the ecstasy I was about to feel.

Omar's big strong hands spread my ass cheeks apart and he began to fuck my ass with his tongue viciously. I swear this man eats ass better than any man I have ever crossed paths with. I felt my orgasm building already and he hadn't even been eating for a good two minutes. The way he thumbed around with my clit while still eating my ass caused my legs to buckle. Thank goodness I was leaned over the couch, or I would've fallen flat on my face.

"Fuck Zaddy, I'm bout to cum. Oh, my goodness, I'm bout to cum! FUCKKKKK!" I yelled as he continued to devour me from behind.

"Throw that ass back on this tongue. Umm hmm, just like that!" Omar was able to get out between me throwing my ass back on his face. I started making my ass clap to the best of my ability, because the pleasure was so great my concentration was all fucked up.

"AHHHH. UMM Ummmm." I moaned aloud as I felt my juices spilling down the inside of my legs. Omar wasted no time getting up from his knees, flipping me over, and inserting his rock hard dick inside of me. Halfway hanging over the couch, I used my hands to hold on for leverage. Omar started beating it up in a circular motion and I could hear my pussy smacking as if he was playing in a small puddle of water.

"Shit Tini, this shit so fucking good!" Omar confessed as he used his free hand that wasn't holding onto my hip to grab my neck. He knew that choking shit turned me on even more. His big frame and husky hands were so fucking sexy it's sickening. I used my pussy muscles to massage his dick while still inside of me and began to rotate my hips in half circles while he continued to pump in and out of me. Omar stopped and began to lick on my clit, only causing me to cum again back-to-back. The moment he felt my cum escape my body, he stood up again and begin to fuck me like before. Getting fucked and sucked like this, how could any woman get tired of it.

"Tini I'm bout to nut, where you want it?" Omar questioned, I sat up, climbed off the back of the sofa and dropped to my knees. I mean shit, the way he eats this pussy and ass, how can I not allow him to release in my mouth.

I sucked his dick inside of my mouth without any hands and begin to tighten my jaws for the suction effect. Sucking while using my tongue to twirl around his dick, I knew his nut was coming soon. As I increased my speed and began to gag on his dick from deep throating him, I felt the warm liquid begin to go down my throat. I continued to suck until he was completely limp.

"Tini, why can't I nut inside of you? We been fucking for a year and you still act like you scared I'm goin get you pregnant or something." Omar said, and I brushed him off as if I hadn't heard his last comment.

"What, you don't like me swallowing your nut or something?" I asked with sarcasm in my voice and headed to my bedroom, so I could hop in the shower.

"Your ass always got something smart to say. What nigga wouldn't like that shit. I'm just saying. You be quick to jump up when I say I'm bout to nut." Omar yelled in the direction of my bedroom.

"Shut up talkin shit and come get in the shower!" I yelled back to him. Omar wasted no time coming to join me in the shower.

The moment he got in behind me, I knew we were getting ready to start round two. Wrapping his arms around my waist and beginning to toy with my pussy, I felt another orgasm coming on that quick. I turned to face him and wrapped my arms around his neck. He knew that meant I wanted to be picked up and he did as I desired. Picking me up and pinning me against the wall with my legs wrapped around him was by far my favorite position. Omar gave me slow, deep long strokes against the wall of the shower. The hot steamy water combined with the sounds of our sex topped any porno I've ever watched.

After the session we had in the shower, the both of us were wore the fuck out. It's something about having sex in the water that drains the life out of me. Thank goodness for these bundles being wet and wavy, because I for damn sure wouldn't have had the energy to straighten them. I grabbed some yoga pants and a tank top before heading to the living room to get the dress Omar tore off me.

"Where the fuck you think you going with them skin tight pants and tank top barely reaching your ass?" Omar walked into the room talking shit as he was getting himself dressed.

"I'm not going anywhere besides my sisters'. You act like you can see my pussy or something." I fussed back. That little jealous shit was cute to me, but I had to pretend to be nonchalant.

"Shit, might as well be able to. I can see the whole print. How would you feel if I walked around in basketball shorts letting my dick just swag for muthafuckas to see?"

"First off, that's no comparison. Secondly, you don't like basketball shorts, so I wouldn't have to worry about that."

"How you know what I like? Shit, just cause you haven't seen me rocking them doesn't mean I don't like them." Omar, of course, had to be difficult.

"Please! You can't fool me. If you liked something, you would wear it. Bottom line. The only reason I'm leaving the house in the first place is to go pick up an order for you. Had you not ordered them damn edibles, I would've been in the house for the remainder of the evening."

"Well since you put it that way, just make sure you don't make any pitstops in the tight ass leggings or whatever y'all call 'em. Pick up my shit and back here. You got it?" Omar said in a serious tone. I knew he was serious, but he had to be tripping if he thought I would really go elsewhere dressed like this. I didn't even have a bra on. Don't get me wrong, I got some perky little titties, but still.

I gave Omar a kiss on the lips and headed towards the door to my garage.

"Just set the alarm when you leave. I'm going run over to Deja and Dreia's. I'm sure you'll be gone before I get back, so I'll just see you later or something."

I gave Omar the space he needed for the most part because I know how the streets can be. He's not a block boy, but he runs a large cartel and doesn't need me on his case twenty-four seven. I give him just enough space to roam, but not too much to roam.

"Look at you looking like you just got the shit fucked outta you and walked straight outta the house." Deja joked the moment I walked into their front door.

"And for your information, I did. How bout dat!" I said as I stuck my tongue out in her direction.

"Ewww, like really, we didn't need to know that. I hope you washed up before you came out. Shit, you could've put a bra on too, nasty." Dreia said with her nose scrunched up.

"I know you ain't talkin Dreia, you been getting dicked down something crazy too. Don't act like I ain't hear you coming in late night last night. Umm hmm." Deja said to Dreia and Dreia walked away as if she was busted.

"Everybody just fucking and I'm over here like where the bottle. I need some dick, but I ain't got the time for these lame ass niggas. It seems like every nigga gotta agenda I ain't trying to follow. I mean a bitch ain't trying to fall in love, but damn!" Dej said as she let out a sigh of frustration.

"Oh, shut the hell up. You only in there talkin shit cause you been drinking that damn Patrón since you woke up, hoe!" Dreia yelled to the living room from the kitchen.

"Oh whatever, fuck you too! I'm just speaking the facts about my life, nobody asked for your input!" Dej said. I couldn't help but laugh. I knew she was buzzing the moment I walked in and she was slurring talking shit. That's my baby sister and I love her whole life, one thing I don't have to worry about is her not speaking her mind or the truth.

Dreia came back to the living room with my order, or should I say Omar's order, cause I for damn sure didn't eat those things.

"Now run me my money, please and thank you. I gotta get ready I'm bout to go to dinner." Dreia said before holding her hand out in my face like a damn panhandler.

"How much I owe you, sis? I been doing so much I don't remember." I told her honestly as I grabbed my phone, so I could sent it to her from the Zelle thing on the Chase banking app.

"You don't owe me. Whoever the order is for owes me $280." she joked while wiggling her fingers in my face.

"Well you know what I meant. They gave me the cash, but I didn't even bring my purse with me, so I'm going send it to your account like I did before. Is that coo?"

"Yeah, that's fine. Any form of payment works for me. And if you run across some customers that have food stamps, that would be great too. I mean, I know one of them parents that have kids at your center get stamps."

"Is you crazy? I ain't bout to be advertising you sell weed snacks at the center." We all started laughing cause that basically what she was telling me to do.

"I mean, you can discreetly pass the word. I know one of them bitches get high. You got too many damn hood kids for their parents to be sober."

"Shit, the order I place weekly for the customers I do get orders from you for should be enough. I know I ain't the only person getting orders."

Dreia didn't know who the large orders that I placed weekly were for, but she knows they spend no less than two hundred every trip. So two hundred times two or three people just from me, I know she had to be making a killing off those shits.

"Ok ok, you're right. I guess I can't be greedy since what I'm doing isn't technically legal in the state of Ohio yet."

Dreia headed upstairs to get ready for wherever she was about to go, while Dej and I chopped it up for a little while before I took my ass home. I needed to catch up on this damn show I was watching called *13 Reasons Why* before Omar called trying to link up for the night.

SIX

ROMEO

As many times as I've said I would never chase a bitch, that's exactly what I found myself doing when it came to Little Miss Deja. Something about her, a nigga had to have. I don't harass her or no shit like that, but I find myself going to Club Onyx every chance I get, in hopes of running into her. I've caught her a couple of times, but not every time. I make sure she's my waitress and I keep it professional, but today is going to be the day I let her know to stop playing games with a nigga. A man like me doesn't have to beg, plead, or chase any female cause I can have any I want, but damn.

I got that Patrón in my system and I'm on it with shawty. The moment she came over to my table today, I damn near pulled her down on my lap, so I could rap in her ear for a second. But I didn't. Instead, I played it coo and waited until now. I noticed it was getting near the end of her shift, because she made her rounds to check on everyone she was serving one last time before walking in my direction.

"Deja, before you come give me the spill about you ending your shift, like you did everyone else, can I talk to you?" I asked with a slur in my tone.

"Yeah, what's up Romeo? Is there something wrong?" she asked in an innocent tone.

"Nah baby, I'm coo." I said as she took a seat next to me in the booth.

"Well, what's up?" she asked in the most naïve way, as if she didn't know I was on her heels.

"What's up with you playing so hard to get? Like, I've never come out of pocket at you, or been on no funny shit. So why you give me such a hard time about exchanging numbers with you? I'm just trying to get to know you, nothing major baby." I noticed when I asked my question she was at a loss for words for a second before she responded to me.

"Honestly Romeo, I honestly hadn't taken you serious. I've watched women flock around you and your brothers. I know a lot about y'all, contrary to your belief, and I don't have time to be another chick looking stupid dealing with you."

"See, that's where you're wrong. You see women flock around us, but how many do you see us flaunt around with? You can't answer that, because you've never seen it. I'm not surprised that you do hear shit about us. I mean, who don't know of the Jones brothers around this bitch? but that doesn't mean that I'm bad news. Until you personally get to know me, how can you be so sure you don't want any dealing with me?"

"You're right. You have a point. I'm just letting you know I'm not cut for games or foolery, so I avoid them by any means." she said as she retrieved her phone from her purse to decline an incoming call.

"Ok, and neither am I. So while you have that phone in your hand, go ahead and put my number in that bitch. Better yet, call me now so I have your number for myself, in case you try to not contact me." I recited my number to Deja and she sent a text to my phone that second.

"Happy now?" Deja asked with a smile on her face.

"Yep, I sure am. Now I can get out of here when you clock out." I said and we both laughed.

"Bye, Romeo."

"Talk to you later, Deja." I said and gave her a smirk.

Instead of going straight home, I stopped by Shadeia's place so she could stop blowing me the fuck up about seeing her. She is the most aggravating bitch I have ever come in contact with, but that mouth of hers is worth hella cash. She sucks dick like she in a marathon. I have yet to cross paths with a head doctor on her level. I decided to turn my phone on vibrate the moment I pulled up to Shadeia's place.

I knocked on the door and before I could get my hand back down to my side, Shadeia was opening the door butt ass naked. As drunk as I was, I wasn't trying to fuck this bitch today. Some head was the most she could offer me right now.

"Hey, baby!" Shadeia greeted me with a tight embrace.

"What's up? What all this about. Who said I was coming over here for some pussy, freak!" I joked with her.

"Never said you were, but you never said you weren't either. Why not take my chances? I miss that big dick. Why you being all stingy and shit lately? I gotta beg you to come see me. It's not like I know where you stay to come see you."

What she needed to know was with the behaviors she be on, she would never find out where I stay. She's the type of bitch that will pop up to a nigga's crib if he ain't answering her calls, and that type of nonsense I do not have time for.

"Nah, you just be doing the most and I've warned you before I don't have time for all the extras. You act like a nigga put a title on us or something. When you get to pullin little stunts like we together and the most we've ever done was fuck, it's a problem for me. So until you understand that friendships have boundaries, I gotta cut you off from this supply of dope dick, hun. Sorry!" I said and the look on her face was priceless. She acted like she was shocked I said some shit like that to her.

"Romeo, why you gotta be so rude? I never said we were together, but damn I can't show you attention and love when I do see you."

"I'm not saying you can't, but don't put on no show like you my woman. I chose not to call you out while in public cause I don't wanna embarrass you. But it needs to be said at some point, cause I notice the shit is becoming more and more each encounter."

"I'm sorry baby! It won't happen again. Now can I suck your dick?" she asked as she got on her knees and begin to unbuckle my belt. I wasn't going stop her. Shit, I could use some head right about now.

After Shadeia sucked the soul out my dick, I got the fuck outta there without penetrating her or even a conversation for that ass. That Patrón gets me on some other shit, and Shadeia just ain't where it's at right about now. I wanted to head in for the evening, but something told me to hit up Deja and see where her head was.

"Hello?" Deja answered the phone in her normal, innocent tone.

"What's up, Miss Deja? You busy?" I asked hoping like hell she wouldn't say yes.

"Nothing much. Chilling here playing Spades with my Sisters and mom."

"Oh, ok. I can call you back later if I'm interrupting."

"Nah you coo, we ending the game now. What's up with you?"

"Nothing, was about to head home but I decided to call you and see what you were up to first. Can I see you tonight?"

"Um depends, I'm still in my work clothes, so I'm not dressed to be going out anywhere."

"Nah, we can meet up somewhere just to talk and get to know each other. Whatever you're comfortable with."

"That's coo. Where you wanna meet at?"

"We can meet at a park and walk the trail if you not scared." I joked, but many women are scared to walk in the park at night or scared of some fucking bugs.

"Scared of what?" Deja asked with a serious tone.

"Shit, I don't know. Women be scared of every damn thing."

"Sorry, hun, I'm not your typical chick. There's not much in life I fear." When she said that something told me she was dead ass serious.

"Glad to know that. Well, meet me at Hoover Dam in like fifteen to twenty minutes if that's coo."

"Yeah that's fine. I'll meet you there." she said and ended our call.

I headed to Hoover Dam to meet up with Deja and hoped like hell a nigga didn't reek of alcohol and weed. I drank that whole bottle of Patrón at the bar and faced a blunt on the way to Shadeia's crib. Then I lit another one the moment I got back in the car. *Fuck it, I* thought to myself. *Shit, she can either respect it or check it. This is me!*

He can't love you like I love you
Baby, you know it too
And you should never wanna be with a man
If he can't be a man
And do the things to you like I can

The sounds of Jagged Edge *He Can't Love You* filled the speakers of my Camaro as I waited impatiently for Deja to pullup. I sent her a text letting her know I was in a yellow Camaro, so she would know what car to look for and she replied saying she would be here shortly. When Deja pulled up, I wasted no time powering off my car and exiting so I could meet her at hers. Just as she explained, she had on the same outfit as when I saw her earlier today. Which in my opinion was fine, because she had on normal clothes if you asked me. A tank, some ripped jeans, and some sneakers looked sexy as fuck on her small frame. Deja puts you in the mind frame of Taraji P Henson with her sexy ass. She was the exact same skin complexion. Her natural hair was long and flowing down her back and she had the round face. Baby's body was to die for. With a slim waist and fat ass, I can't help but stare when she walks. Her titties aren't big, but they fit her small, petite frame well.

I took the lead on the trail we would be walking. Deja surprisingly started the conversation without any hesitation. I took her for being the shy type because she's always so polite and innocent sounding, but she's actually the complete opposite. Something I can tell just by her conversation and demeanor is that's she not timid or scary, which I can appreciate because of my personality.

"Where do you see yourself in five years?" Deja questioned me and surprisingly I had never thought about the shit until now.

"Damn, you kind of caught me off-guard with that question. Keeping it one thousand, I never really thought about my life that far in advance." I had to keep it real with her, so I wouldn't sound stupid as I thought about it and gave her my answer.

"Well now that I've made you think about it, what comes to mind. What are your goals? Long term goals, I mean."

"I eventually want to start a family of my own. Seeing that I'm twenty-five now, by thirty I wanna be settled down and with at least one kid. I'm sure my money will be long enough to step away from the game and travel the world. What are your goals? Where do you see yourself in five years?" I gave the best answer I could.

"I want to own and operate my own club. I wanna be married and honestly, I never thought about having any kids. I just can't picture myself having any kids. I'll be twenty-eight, so the goal is to be in the process of closing on my first home or owning my own home."

"So, do you not want any kids, or you just never thought about having any? How many siblings do you have total?"

"It's not that I don't want any, I just never pictured myself being a mother. Right now, I'm enjoying living. I enjoy being able to get up and go as I please. I drink a lot and I can't be drunk trying to take care of no kid. I have two sisters. That's it, that's all. How many kids total do you want?

"Shit, I want a big ass family fa real. I want at least five kids. You think you can push out five babies for me?"

"Ha! You crazy. I don't think my body can handle all that." Deja said while giggling.

We continued to walk and talk until we couldn't walk any further on the trail. Then we proceeded to walk back to the cars. By the time we reached our cars, it was a little after two in the morning. Our chemistry and vibe were so right, I wasn't ready to call it a night. The only reason I allowed our night to end was because she had to work tomorrow. Had she been off, I would've tried to keep her out a little longer. Even if it was to just grab a bite to eat so I could stay in her company a little longer.

When we said our goodbyes, I told her to text me and let me know she made it in safe, but she told me she had something better in mind. As we pulled off, she called my phone and we talked until she made it home safe and prepared for bed. Her conversation never had a dry moment. Normally, I'm not a talking on the phone type of nigga, but Deja held my attention with little effort. The conversation flowed so easily.

THIS MORNING my pops called us over to have a meeting. Normally when he calls us for a meeting it's because of something about money or a shipment. But today I just had a gut feeling that it was about to be something else involved. The moment I got to The Slab, Mar and Jul were pulling up at the same time. Walking inside, Bones greeted us and told us that Pops was out back on the patio. We all headed out there and the look of stress was written all over his face.

It's not much that causes my pops to be stressed out, so when he is I know it's a problem. In my twenty-five years of living, I have only witnessed him worried maybe three times, total. In my eyes there was nothing my pops couldn't handle, I hoped to be half the man he is when I get his age. He raised me and my brothers alone, without the help of a mother, and we all turned out damn good.

We all took our seats around the small table that held glasses and a bottle of Rosé. My pops may be old, but he still fucks with the drinking shit. That's something he probably will never give up. He used to smoke weed back in the day when we were younger, but he stopped a couple years back. We all grabbed our cups and took our drinks to the head. It's almost like we all could feel something wasn't right from his demeanor.

"I'm not gone waste no time or beat around the bush on why I called y'all over here. We got a problem, and for once I can honestly say I don't know how we going handle it." Hearing him say that caused my eyebrows to raise. He had me curious as fuck. I poured myself another cup of Rosé and sat back to hear what the fuck was going on.

"Y'all know me and my brother Ramaro never saw eye-to-eye, which is one of the main reasons I moved to the States so early on. But that's neither here nor there. He's taken over the streets of Haiti and feels it's time for him and his sons to move here in the States. But the problem doesn't come in until I found out he has basically started interfering with our connect. His oldest son was just recently released from prison, and connected him to a half son that Ramaro never claimed. I guess since he's expanding territory, he reunited with them both. Both of his sons live here in the States already. Surprisingly they both live in Ohio as well. Had I known this, I would've been put the word in y'all ear, but I'm just getting wind of this."

"So, what's up? What's the nigga's names? Are they people on our camp? Is it smoke? Let me know!" I said, sitting up on the edge of my seat. I'm always ready for war whenever, wherever. Especially when it comes to my family.

"Now wait a minute, and calm down, brah." Mar tried to reason with me because he knew just how fast I could go from zero to one thousand.

"I honestly don't know where Ramaro's head is at, but I'm sure it's on some bullshit because he's messing with our connect. The oldest sons name is Kenneth and the other one is Kamar. I don't wanna jump the gun too soon, because just as much power as we have, so does Ramaro. So with him connecting with his sons they will have that very same power. This can turn into a deadly situation and I wanna make sure our every move is thought out first."

The look on Jul and Mars face showed they were ready for war, but they were waiting on Pops' go. Me, on the other hand, I wasn't trying to wait. I needed to do some homework of my own to figure out who these muthafuckas were out here in the streets, and what type of weight their names held.

After Pops said what he had to say, he got up and went in the house. Normally, that's what he does when he's done, he removed himself from the conversation and goes on about his business. We all took that as the closing of the meeting and headed out as well. We all had a lot to think about, so no one said a word to each other. Hopping in my truck, I couldn't even turn my music up and zone out. I needed to get something stronger than the Rosé in my system to keep me calm. I'm ready to see some bloodshed and have my pops at ease again.

The fucked up part about all of this is Ramaro and my pops were close from the stories he used to tell us. It wasn't until their father was killed and the throne was to be run by one of them. Instead of splitting it like me and my brothers do everything, Ramaro wanted everything and my pops wasn't going. He damn near was at war with his own flesh and blood over the money and fame in Haiti. Pops told us he would've stayed and fought it out until the death, but Mar was born, and he didn't want to take that risk with his firstborn involved. Ramaro and Pops didn't have the same mother, so that's where a lot of the confusion stemmed from, but didn't come out until our grandfather was murdered.

Growing up, it was instilled in us to never allow money, fame, or greed get in between us. Whatever one of us had, all three had and whenever we came into something, we split that shit evenly. I could never see myself going at either of my brother's necks over no shit like that. It's just not in us. I needed to find these two cats that were cousins by blood, but enemies by default to see exactly where their heads were at. Who's to say they would be on the same shit their father was on.

I had plans on going to the liquor store and taking my ass home, but somehow, I ended up at Club Onyx. I guess I could get my bottle from there and see my Deja all at the same time.

SEVEN

DREIA

I don't know what it is, but why does it seem like the moment you start to get over a person and move forward, they wanna come back into your life and make shit right. Lately Kamar had been showing me a completely different side to him that he should've shown me years ago. As bad as I wanted to see how much of the change was permanent, I didn't want to take the risk of being hurt yet again by the same man. There's no way I would be able to forgive myself if I allowed him to play me again after moving forward and finally meeting someone new that I actually like. Julian has yet to give me a reason to cut him off, but Kamar was making it really hard.

I still do business with Kamar, so it's hard to cut him off completely. Then to top it off, he stops by the house and randomly brings me shit. Like, where the hell was this man when we were together. I thought he would've caught the hint that I wasn't fooling with him by now. I haven't had sex with Kamar since I started sleeping with Julian. Kamar doesn't know about Julian, and Julian knows only of Kamar, but not who he is, and I want to keep it like that. Kamar has a horrible temper and I'm not trying to have him and Julian at each other's head over me. Not saying Julian and I are close enough for all that, but Kamar coming at him will only result in retaliation.

Julian and I have been taking things slow between us. The ball is always in my court and he knows that I'm not trying to rush into anything right now. I fear getting hurt again, which I know shouldn't stop me from allowing another man to show me different, but it does. Julian gives me just the amount of space I need, so I'm ok with the pace things are going. I feel somewhat bad because Julian is ready for the next step, and that I can tell just by the things he says. But I don't want either of us to get hurt as a result of doing such. He's a wonderful person, don't get me wrong, but everyone has skeletons. Just recently, he took me to meet his father. I was shocked to see his father was still young and hip at his age. I guess that's what having all sons does to you. I'm not saying that Miss Maris is old and out of fashion or anything, because she isn't. But she's definitely more laid back than Julian's parent.

With all the information I had to learn about Julian, I didn't learn about him being Haitian until I met his dad and I asked about his strong accent. I kind of figured because I heard him speak a little bit of Creole while on the phone while I was present. Miss Maris is Haitian as well, so I could make out some of what he was saying. Growing up in a household with a woman who is Haitian, you'll pick up certain shit. Omar Sr sat out back talking and that's when he explained to me that his father was born and raised in Haiti. Julian never spoke much about his childhood or his mother, so I never asked. I just waited until he told me things. His dad, on the other hand, was a social butterfly. He told me all about Haiti and when he first moved to the United States after Omar, his oldest son, was born.

I didn't even know that Julian and his brothers grew up in Texas and moved here after the boys started getting into too much shit at a young age down there. I was happy to have met his father, because he was very warm and welcoming. I have plans on introducing Julian into Miss Maris, but not until the time is right and we make something more official than what we are. Shit, it took Kamar no time to meet Miss Maris, and you see how that shit played out.

Being around Julian's father gave me an understanding of why he and his brothers were so close. Their father is a family-oriented man and speaks very highly of his sons. Omar Sr gave me a tour of his home and I was in awe. I couldn't believe he stayed in such a big, lavish home all alone. The six bedrooms were all nicely decorated as if there were a guest on the way to enjoy them, which I'm sure has never happened. He had staff members around his home at our beck and call. It's like I was around royalty being in his presence, yet he was still so humble. Julian's home was huge and nice as well, but he didn't have any staff members. Well, none that I knew of anyways. Certain areas of the house were so nice I didn't want to step foot in them, but Mr. Jones insisted. I had a hard time refraining from calling him Mr. Jones, as well. Out of respect for my elder, I automatically called him Mr., but he assured me that he would much rather I call him Omar or Pops.

After we left Mr. Omar's home, we grabbed a bite to eat from Netty's Kitchen. She had some of the best soul food in Columbus for reasonable prices. Julian had got me hip to her and now I'm hooked. He ordered her meatloaf with double mac and cheese and cornbread. I got fried whiting fish with greens, mac and cheese and cornbread as well. Normally, I don't like cornbread, but there's something different about hers. It has a cinnamon and sugar taste to it that you can't resist. Instead of going home, we headed back to Julian's place to watch some damn movie he has been telling me to watch call 2Eleven. Normally I'm not beat for watching them hood movies cause I can't get into them, but if that's what he wanted to do, I'm willing because he's always willing to do whatever I want to.

Julian rolled his blunt and I hit it a couple of times, but not too many. Just enough so he would stop trying to pass it to me. I was already feeling sleepy after I ate all that food, then to top it off, we watched not only 2Eleven but Buff Up. Both movies stared Murda Pain, some actor slash rapper from Detroit I had heard nothing about until Julian put me on game. When it came to rapping and shit, I'm the furthest from hip. I just keep up with what comes on the radio. From time-to-time while I was with Kamar, I would listen to the shit he played in the car, but that was mainly Gotti or MoneyBagg Yo.

Laying across Julian's lap while he massaged the upper part of my back, I felt myself drifting off to sleep until I heard Julian clear his throat.

"Babe, you sleep?" Julian said in a low tone.

"No, what's up hunny?" I lied cause I for sure had fallen asleep.

"We been kicking it now and I'm ready to officially make you mine. How you feel about that?" Julian caught me off-guard and I didn't know how to respond. It's not that I didn't like him or see potential in him, it's just I don't know if I'm ready to be in another relationship so soon.

"Babe, what's on your mind? How you feel? What you think?"

"Jul, I want to say ok and I'm with being your woman, but I just don't know."

"What don't you know, exactly? What makes you so hesitant?"

"I don't know if I can be in another relationship right now. So soon. I still have trust issues and issues from my past relationship that I haven't dealt with yet." The best thing to do was be truthful with him so that's what I did.

"Ok and I understand that. I see that shit in you, but how will you ever deal with it or get over it if you don't try. The first step you've already made by moving forward and dealing with me period. I'm not in the business of running game on you or playing with your heart. I know you've probably heard these things before, but if I only wanted to toy around with you and your heart, I could've done that from the gate." Julian said and continued to smoke his blunt.

"You're right, Jul. I mean, I'm not against it, but I'm just skeptical. I mean, we can't try to make something between us work, I guess." I said and shrugged my shoulders some.

"What the fuck you mean try to make something between us work? Do you realize that we basically are together, just without the title as of now? So why not make it official?" Jul chuckled and so did I, because he had a very valid point.

"You're right. So I guess it's official, I'm Julian Jones' woman." I said and he started laughing at me like I said a damn joke.

"You so silly!" Julian said before leaning down and giving me a kiss behind my left ear.

After our conversation, I made a mental note of all the things that I needed to do and end everything that was going on between Kamar and I. No, we aren't having sex, but the ties are still too close. Especially now, since I'm officially no longer single. I don't want to change my phone number for the sake of my business, but his ass is for sure going on the block list after I tell him that we are done on the business side and he is no longer allowed over. Never really cut Kamar off before, I can only imagine how this is going to go.

LAST NIGHT I didn't sleep as well as I normally do whenever I'm over Julian's. My mind was all over the place. A part of me started to question the decision I made by agreeing to a relationship. The other part of me felt like I did the right thing. I mean, Julian is a sweetheart and has yet to make me feel a certain type of way about anything. But all the what-ifs ran through my head. I didn't want to put in in the same boat as Kamar, but those are the very same things that crossed my mind. On top of Kamar's reaction. Today when I woke up, Julian brought me home early so I could get the orders out that needed to be completed for this weekend. Kamar was supposed to come to do a drop off with my products within the next hour, and that's when I'm going to tell him this will be my last time I need his services or help. I'm just going to have to talk to Julian about getting me a connect. I mean, it's not like he didn't already know the business I did, it's just he didn't know who my supplier was.

I heard the doorbell and I knew it was Kamar, so I prepared myself for the conversation we were about to have.

"What's up, baby?" Kamar greeted me as I opened the door. When he reached out to me to give me a hug and neck kiss as he usually does, I tried to turn to avoid it, but without making it seem obvious.

"Nothing much. Just getting these orders ready. I need to talk to about some stuff, though," I said, trying to hurry up and get what I needed to say off my chest.

"What's up baby, you straight?" Kamar asked with a raised eyebrow.

"Yeah, I'm coo. Nothing major. This is going to be my last order from you, though."

"Why, what's wrong? I thought business was going good."

"It is. I just feel like it's that time that I finally stop this thing that we have between us. Like, you know how we still stayed in contact even after breaking up. All the popping up and random calls or texts. Everything between us, I feel it's finally time for it to stop. No hard feelings or anything, it's just that time, Kamar." I rushed and said everything I needed to before I lost the courage to do so.

"Wait, so what you saying is basically you cutting me off. I thought we was going work on us and getting back together. So, what your telling me basically is you fucking someone new. Who is the nigga?" Kamar was getting agitated, I could tell by the tone of his voice. But he was definitely tripping if he thought what we had between us was actually us taking steps to getting back together.

"No, I'm not saying it's a new nigga. Why do men always jump to conclusions and think it's a new man when it's time for a woman to let go? When we originally broke up, I did say we could work towards getting back together, but Kamar that was months ago. I mean honestly, we haven't had sex in months and it's time. I'll always have love for you. I just need to move forward in life and us doing business won't make it easy." Hell no, I didn't want to come out and say I'm fucking with Julian Jones, so I worded it to the best of my ability.

"That bullshit and you know it. What we have between us should never interfere with your money. I don't give a fuck what you say, I know it's a new nigga and when I find out, I'mma handle that nigga. Dreia, you're gone be my wife one day, and right now we just need a break to get ourselves together."

This nigga had definitely taken a hit of the wrong blunt this morning if he thought that at this point I looked forward to marrying his hoe ass. If he can't stay faithful to me while we are only in a relationship, what the fuck makes me think he will in marriage. Then to top it off, over this thing he considers a short break, he hasn't even improved. I can count on one hand the number of days or dates in which we spent quality time before I met Julian. That along showed me he wasn't focused on us anymore, but more so himself.

"Kamar, I don't know if you remember or not, but you are the reason we aren't together. So sayin WE need to work on ourselves is wrong. We separated because YOU couldn't be faithful. Not ME, BUT YOU!" I didn't mean to raise my voice, but this nigga was trippin and I needed him to know I wasn't beat for the shit today.

"Whatever Dreia. Here go your shit. We'll see!" Kamar dropped my package on the floor and turned to walk toward the door. "Oh, and I'm dead ass serious when I say I'mma handle whoever the nigga is you dealing with. You gone see, just watch."

Kamar's bitch ass attitude had just pissed me clean off. It's over and has been between us, so I don't know what the fuck his problem was. I mean, he acts like I was going sit around forever and wait for him to see what was right in front of him all along. Fuck outta here. He got another thing coming if he thinks he's gone run up or ever confront Julian over me, Julian ain't that type. I won't lie like Kamar is some punk ass nigga, but he will definitely meet his match fucking around with Julian. Just the stories I've heard about him and his brothers is enough evidence to know he's not going allow the shit.

I rushed to lock the door back behind him. On the way to the kitchen, I grabbed my phone to send Julian a quick text asking him was he available. I needed to talk to him now or never about needing his help with supply, as well the threats Kamar made. I would hate for him to be caught by the element of surprise whether Kamar knows for sure or not who I'm dealing with. Julian and I don't hide, we go on dates and spend quality time in public often. Julian texted me back letting me know he was free and would stop by since he was in the area.

It wasn't even ten minutes before Julian was sending a text letting me know he was pulling up. I made sure to turn the oven on low because I didn't want my shit to burn while I was having this conversation with him. I don't know Julian's moods like that as of yet, so I don't know how he's going to respond. I just hope it's not on no bullshit like Kamar was. Rushing to the front door to open it, I took a deep sigh and prepared myself.

"Hey, baby!" Jul greeted me with a kiss on the lips.

"Hey!" I cooed back.

"You straight? How the orders coming along?" Jul questioned me.

"Yes, I'm fine, but I need to talk to you about a few things. Some on the business side, some on the relationship tip. The orders are coming, I'm still completing them actually. I just turned the oven down some so they wouldn't burn."

"Ok baby, talk to me. What's on your mind? Let's talk business first. You wanna talk right here, or we need to go to another room?" Julian asked.

"No, right here is fine. Dej gone somewhere." I replied. Julian took a seat and gave me his undivided attention. "Ok, so the first thing being business. You know the type of business I do and the type of supplies I use. Up until my last order of supplies, my ex was my connect, so I never had to actually go out and find one. Paying for my product isn't the problem, but now that we have officially made it official, I don't want to have any ties to him out of respect for you. So, I wanted to know if you knew someone or have access to large quantities of weed. The type of weed does really matter, because the treats are strong either way." I looked at Julian's face for his reaction, but I couldn't read him.

"Oh, well first let me say I appreciate you not only respecting me, but our relationship as well by deading that shit between y'all whether it was business or not. I'm your man, so it's my responsibility to be your support and help where needed. As long as we are together, there will never be a need for another man to help with anything. I can promise you that. Getting your products for you will be no problem, and money isn't an issue baby, and you should already know that. When you say large quantities, how much you talking? How frequently do you need the shit?"

"Umm maybe like a pound and a half?" I said while shrugging my shoulders with my hands raised.

"Awww baby, I thought you were talkin large numbers. A pound and a half ain't shit. But you never said how often you need it and do you need some right now?" Julian said what I needed wasn't shit like it was a small amount. That shit caused my eyes to become enlarged. I thought a pound was a lot of shit. Kamar always made it seem like it was a big deal.

"Well babe, to me it is a large amount. I don't know what you're used to, but twenty-two hundred dollars' worth of weed is a lot to me. Granted it makes me more than what I spend, that's still a lot of weed. I normally go through that amount in about a week, or a week in a half, it depends on the number of orders I get. Around the holidays it's a little less than a week. I got my last bulk from him today, so I won't need any more for at least a week."

"That's not a problem, baby. I'll make sure you have it before the week is up. Now about the relationship talk, what's on your mind?"

"Wait babe, do you need the money now or when you bring it to me? I normally pay him in advance, so either way works for me."

"You ain't hear nothing I just said, did you. I told you money isn't the issue. You're my woman and I'm supporting your business and hustle. What the fuck I look like taking money from you when you're trying to build? I mean, I understand a couple thousand may not be a low price, but that's nothing to give to the woman I'm trying to build with. That amounts not gone make or break me, baby!"

"Ok ok. I was listening, but I just want to make sure we are on the same page. I don't want it to seem like because we are officially a couple, I'm just coming to you now with my hand out cause that's never the case."

"Nah, I don't think that at all. You good, baby. Now back to this relationship topic."

I liked the way the conversation between Julian and I was flowing. He's so much more mature about shit than what Kamar is and easier to talk to.

"Ok, I didn't technically tell my ex I was in a relationship. However, I did tell him we are cutting ties and I don't want contact with him any longer, so there's no need for him to come to visit, call my phone, or none of that. Of course, he assumed it was because of a new nigga. He said a few slick comments and I just want to be upfront with you. Because although he doesn't know who you are, or if I am for sure involved with someone else, he's not happy about it. I just don't want there to ever be no shit between y'all and it's over me or my fault for not telling you."

Julian's face scrunched up some.

"What you mean he wasn't happy. Y'all ain't been together you were single when I'm met you. Y'all ain't fucking around, cause I know how that pussy fits my shit. Plus, I trust you that much. If I didn't, I wouldn't have made you my woman. Your ex-nigga ain't a problem you gotta worry about. That's for me to handle if he gets out of place. You spoke your peace to him, now if he can't accept that I'll deal with him. What's this niggas name anyway?"

"His name is Kamar. He's a hustla, so you may have heard of him before. He's from the north side, but he's all over because of his line of work."

When I said that name I noticed his entire face and mood shifted some.

"Umm hmmm. Ok ok. Yeah, don't you worry about none of that. Was that all as far as this relationship talk, baby? I told my brothers I would meet up with them after I stopped to see what was up with you."

"Yeah, that's it, babe."

Julian got up gave me a kiss and headed out the door. After watching him to his car and locking the door back, I headed back to finish up my order before Dej returned, because we were going to Miss Maris' house for dinner tonight. I felt a sense of relief that I told Kamar that we were completely done, and I was honest with Julian about everything. Not only did cutting Kamar off help me to feel more comfortable about being with Julian, it saved me hella money. Spending between eight to ten thousand a month is a lot, but I make double that back. So now that I won't be spending any of that, it's all profit means good things for me.

EIGHT

DEJA

Romeo is something else. Had I known dude would be so coo, I would've been given him my number instead of playing hard to get. He was for damn sure right when he said the things I hear about him and knowing him personally are two different things. Dude is hell on wheels, though. He keeps me laughing whenever we talk or link up. After the first night of us walking and talking, we been linking every day since. He says he's single and he has to be, because the amount that we talk, there's no way a woman would allow her man to.

So far we have done random link ups, breakfast dates, lunch, and dinner. Romeo makes sure to see me at least once a day, on top of talkin or texting me throughout the day. I have yet to have sex with him and I'm honestly not in any rush. I don't want him to think this is any other situation where he can spend a little cash on me and I'mma bust it wide open for him. I can't lie like he doesn't make the kitty purr, cause Romeo is fine as thee fuck, but I just don't want him to place me in a category with every other female he's encountered.

Romeo's caramel skin tone with his shoulder-length sandy brown dreads are enough to turn any female on. Then to top it off, he has green eyes that look hazel some days. I wondered where he got his eyes from, because the other brothers all have brown eyes from what I saw. They are light brown, but not green. He's not short, but he's not tall like his siblings either. Romeo's only stands about five-foot-nine, where his brothers are both over six-feet. Of course, he's taller than me, cause I'm only five-foot-even. But who isn't taller than me? His teeth are pearly white, but he rocks a gold grill on his bottom teeth. When the time does come for us to have sex, best believe I'm gone shine the fuck outta his grill, so I hope he knows what to do when it comes to the head giving department.

I only scheduled to work a half a day because Romeo wanted to go out on a date, and since I normally only have lengthy dates after work, I decided to take some time off. It's not like I ever call off of work any other day, so today wouldn't hurt. He told me it was a surprise, so I told him I would be wearing something comfortable because Romeo is the type of guy that likes being outside. I don't have time to get dressed up all cute in some heels and he wants to go bike riding or some shit like that. The outfit that I wore to work would be the outfit I wore on our date. A PINK sweat suit with a form-fitting tee with my Jordan retro 11's would have to do. Dreia dropped me off at work this morning so that Romeo could pick me up. I had yet to tell her that I was talking to him because I wanted to see where things were going.

Romeo sent me a text message letting me know that he was pulling up. I clocked out, said my goodbyes to a few coworkers, and was outta there. Normally when I see him, he's driving his Camaro, but today we were in his Tahoe. I love big trucks. Hopefully, one day soon, he lets me push this bitch. I look good on the passenger side of any vehicle, but I would look even better behind the wheel.

"Hey, Mr." I greeted him as I stepped into the passenger side of his truck.

"How are you today, Miss?"

"I'm good. Excited to see what you have planned for us today."

"You'll like it, trust me. You're dressed perfect for the occasion, too."

"I see. I'm surprised to see you with a sweat suit on. Normally you got on your fancy designer jeans and expensive shoes."

"So, what you saying? My Nike sweatsuit isn't good enough or my LeBron's don't cost enough," Romeo joked. We held small talk until we got to the COSI parking lot. The first thought that came to my mind was, *I know this nigga ain't bring me to no damn COSI. I am not a kid and I do not want to have a science field trip.* Stepping out the car, I allowed him to take the lead because I didn't have a clue what we were doin or where we were goin.

Romeo grabbed my hand and led me to the Riverfront where there was a small boat waiting for us. I had told him before I wanted to ride on a boat, but I was scared of large bodies of water. I guess this was his way of trying to break me in. When we got on the boat, I noticed there was a picnic-style lunch prepared for us, along with a bottle of Ace of Spades. One thing about Romeo, he likes to drink just as much as I do, and we smoke together. I'm glad he doesn't pass judgment on my extracurricular activities, cause I'm not about to change for anyone. This is me, take it or leave it.

The scenery was beautiful. I've been down to the Riverfront plenty of times because Dreia and I used to come here and walk to exercise, but I've never actually got to see what the entire things look like until today. It's peaceful. Other than the music Romeo was playing on his phone, I could only hear nature and the city. This was for sure a date I wasn't expecting from someone like him, especially the picnic-style lunch. But it's well appreciated.

When he retrieved the pre-rolled blunt from his little bag he packed for our date, I had to warn him I wasn't smoking that entire thing with him today. The last time we smoked a whole blunt of his weed, my ass passed out on him in the movies. Besides, we had already been drinking that Ace of Spades, so I had a nice buzz going. J. Holiday came on and Romeo started singing along.

Lately, I feel like I been slippin, and it's you that got me trippin
I can't control myself when I'm around you, Oh

*With any other I would've been done, Love to left the next one
But I just can't shake you off.*

Listening to R&B music with him is nothing new, because that's all he basically plays when we are in the car. But I never knew he could sing. I don't mind Romeo listening to R&B all the time because that's the music I prefer to hear as well. The only difference is, I can't sing for shit. Hearing the notes he hit with J. Holiday, I couldn't help but to smile. Then when he grabbed my hand, looked me in my eye while singing word for word, I totally forgot I was holding the blunt and smoking because he really caught me off-guard with this move. As the song came to a close, I passed the blunt back to him, although it had gone out a long time ago.

As he lit the blunt again, he looked over at me with one of the cutest smiles ever. I felt myself beginning to blush, no matter how hard I was trying to fight it. I never had a man sing to me, especially not on a serious note. The lyrics of the song made me feel like he was trying to tell me something, but subliminally. I didn't want to jump to conclusions, but that was the giveaway that Romeo was feeling me just as much as I was feeling him.

"Deja, we been kicking it and I can't help but want to feel your presence when you're not around. We click mad well and everything flows so easy without effort. I know when we first started, which wasn't very long ago, we both said we were looking for anything serious right now. But, that's changed. Spending time with you and talking to you, I see I want something more between us. So, I'm going ask you this, and no matter your response, I still want things to remain the way they are between us. Are you ready to be my woman?"

My face probably gave him my answer before I could even respond.

"Yes, baby. I'll be your woman, Romeo."

"Now I'm going tell you this shit now, so I never have to repeat it in the future. Don't fuck around and get somebody killed over you."

"What you mean by that?" I heard all about Romeo's temper, but I've never had to witness it, so him saying this caught me off-guard a little.

"What I mean is you're *my woman!*" He said as he put his hand to his chest. "I know the work you do, but there's levels to certain shit I would tolerate. As long as you respect this relationship, we won't have any problems."

"Ok, I respect that. Just make sure you do the same and we will be straight!"

"Not a problem!" He said before taking a pull from the blunt and looking up into the sky.

After our date was over, I decided it was finally time for Romeo to meet my sisters. I knew both Destini and Dreia were at the house because they were working on some new desserts that Dreia would be adding to her menu that included alcohol. I hoped like hell that they wouldn't be talking shit about me being with Romeo after all the time I curbed him.

Pulling up to my place, Romeo remained seated as if he was just about to drop me off and that's when I told him I wanted him to meet my sisters. Although we were all meeting up here to go have dinner with Miss Maris, we had a little bit of time to play with before we actually got there. I can tell he was happy about it because that sexy grin spread across his face. It's not I was ashamed of him meeting them, I just wanted to make sure he wasn't on no fuck shit before I announced who I was talking to. I know Dreia talks to his brother, but I'm not sure of how serious they are because she hasn't come out and said anything about him. I just notice she's gone a lot more. But leave that shit to Dreia, she could be out with him or Kamar. I'm not callin my sister a hoe, but she been stuck on Kamar for so long, I don't think she will ever let go of his ass one hundred percent. Besides, Kamar still comes by the house from time-to-time and she still does business with him. If her and Julian were anything near serious, I'm sure all that shit would be dead by now.

When we walked into the front door Dreia and Destini were

sitting on the couch, watching TV, talkin. The look on both of their faces was priceless. Like I said, I had never told anyone about Romeo and I talking, so today would be news for the both of them.

"Well hello!" Destini said sarcastically. She knew all of the Jones brothers and about them, but she never spoke much on her opinions of them. Destini being the older sister, I expected her to say something first.

"Hey, Romeo." Dreia spoke.

"Hello, ladies. How y'all been?"

"Good!" They both said in unison.

"Well I wanted to introduce y'all but you both have met him already. So instead, since y'all already know who he is, let me reintroduce Romeo to y'all since we are dating now," I said and gave them a big grin.

"Wait y'all what? When the hell did this happen?" Destini asked.

"Right, that's all I wanna know? Last I knew, y'all never got a chance to exchange numbers. Where I been? How I miss this?" Dreia said sarcastically.

"We been talking for a little minute now. I just hadn't spoke on it until I knew where we were going with everything," I explained to them both while Romeo laughed at their sarcasm.

"Since we making confessions, I guess I'll share mine as well. Julian and I are together as well. I kept it a secret for those very same reasons." Dreia said and my mouth bout hit the floor. Not that I didn't see it coming. I thought she was about to tell us she was back with Kamar, but never Julian. I remember him bringing her home one morning, but that was over a month ago. I hadn't heard anything about him since that day.

"Shit y'all two just spilling all the damn tea today ain't y'all. I guess it's only right to give y'all a dose of my tea as well then." Destini said before picking up her water bottle off the coffee table and taking a sip.

"Omar and I have been talking now for some time now. We are

not technically in a relationship, but that's the man I've been dealing with." She said and took another sip from her water bottle.

"Damn, is it my turn to tell a secret now too?" Romeo joked and we all started laughing. "Nah but fa real though, Destini I been knowing about you and Omar for a nice little minute but that was y'all business, so I wasn't going speak on it if you hadn't." Romeo said, and I nudged him on the side.

"Bae, why you ain't give me a hint or something. Dang!" I pouted as if I was really bothered by him not telling me. It wasn't any of my business technically, but I'm nosey and she is my sister.

We all sat and had small talk for a few minutes before Miss Maris called Destini's phone asking were we on our way. We had totally let it slip our mind while talking that the three of us had prior engagements. We all headed out and I walked over to Romeo's car to give him a kiss goodbye, promising I would call him soon as we finished our dinner date with our mom. I had yet to tell Romeo about my childhood or having a foster mother, but when the time comes, I'll explain it to him.

Walking into Maris' house, the aroma of the food damn near swept me off my feet. I mean, don't get me wrong, me and my sisters can cook. But growing up on Maris' cooking caused my taste buds to be biased. Beside,s I had only eaten that picnic food Romeo prepared for our date earlier, so my stomach was damn near touching my back at this point.

"Maris, what you in here whipping up? Got my stomach ready to cave in!" Destini said the moment she walked through the door.

"Hey, babies. I made some vegetable stew, rice with beans and Poulet Aux Noix." She replied. One thing I can say is if we wanted an authentic Haitian meal, Maris was the one to get it done. The Poulet Aux Noix has always been mine and my sisters' favorite. It's basically just chicken with cashew nuts.

"Ma, is everything done already. I'm so hungry I'm bout to start eating off my acrylic nails." I joked but I was really hungry.

"Yes, everything is done. I'm in here making plates now. Go ahead and get cleaned up and to the table."

Maris always made sure we washed our hands and sat together as a family when we ate dinner. No matter if we ate every other meal outside of the home, when it came to dinner, we all united growing up. Maris never worked and was a stay at home mom, but as we got older, we worked and ran the streets like normal teenage girls do.

Once we all cleaned up, as Maris calls it, we took our seats at the dining room table and prepared for grace and to eat. Maris said grace and we all begin to enjoy our dinner. For the first few minutes, everyone was silent. Other than the utensils touching our plates, we didn't say anything until Maris broke the silence.

"Y'all girls been so busy I haven't talked to you much other than Destini. What's going on? Update me on y'all lives." Maris was always an active parent. If you ask me, she always made sure there was an open line of communication between us.

"Well, I've been busy working and getting my business off the ground. Nothing much other than I finally cut Kamar off and started dating someone new. I'll introduce you to him once I get a feel of where things are going between us. It's still early on and too soon to me." Dreia said.

"I'm thankful you finally let go of Kamar. I've always felt like his mom worked some roots on you or something because you were so tied to him." Maris said. Maris believed in voodoo very strongly and I believe it's because of her Haitian descent.

"I don't know. But if she did, hopefully it's worn off by now cause I've had enough of that man and his ways. It's long overdue. I haven't felt so relieved in some time." Dreia confessed.

"Let's hope. There's no greater feeling than having joy without any burdens breaking you down because of another's choices."

Maris knew all about Kamar's cheating ways and never passed judgment on Dreia for going back to him. She always told us to be mindful of our feelings because they don't dictate others' actions. I didn't understand it as a child, but I do now.

"Same ol' same ol' for me. No new updates here." Destini said while still stuffing her face. I wasn't sure if Maris knew about her and Omar's dealing because shit, we had just found out today. But I wasn't going to speak on it if she didn't.

"How about you, my baby." Maris said and looked in my direction.

"I'm still working and promoting. I've been thinking about taking the next step to opening my own club. I'm supposed to go speak with a loan consultant next week about a building near Onyx. I'm in a relationship now. I want you to meet him, but I need to meet his family first to make sure I'm not getting myself into some mess. After I meet his, I'll let you know. He's a very sweet guy."

"Ok, well don't rush it. When you feel it's right for both situations, you'll know. That goes for the business too, Deja. I really don't want you to take out any loans, so let me know if you need some help. After you go look at the building and go over the details, let me know what they say. As far as the guy's family, you can't always judge a person by their family. So don't let that make or break y'all's relationship."

Maris was right, but I needed to see what type of background Romeo came from. I mean I know of his brothers, but his parents he's never spoken much about, other than when he's on the way to or from his father's house.

We sat and talked for a little while longer as we ate. Shortly after dinner we all packed our to go plates and said our goodbyes. Destini drove us all over to Maris' in her car, so she had to drop me and Dreia back off at home.

I hadn't heard from Romeo since he left my house earlier, so I sent him a text when I got back home seeing what he was up to.

Me: *Hey bae, what you doin?*

Romeo: *Wrapping up some business. Thinking about you. What are you doing?*

Me: *The same thing, thinking about you. I miss you already.*

Romeo: *Is that right? I miss you too baby. You done with your mom?*

Me: *Yeah, we just got back home. I made you a plate in case you want something to eat.*

Romeo: *Thanks, baby. You staying with me tonight?*

Me: *Of course. Text me when you're on the way. I have a late day at work tomorrow, so I don't have to go in until two.*

Romeo: *Bet, I'll text you when I'm pulling up.*

Me: *ok bae see you soon.*

I grab my Jimmy Choo oversized bag and grabbed a few pairs of panties, bras, deodorant, toothbrush, and a set of my favorite Victoria's Secret scent to take with me to Romeo's house. I planned on leaving these things at his house, so I wouldn't have to worry about bringing it over in my purse every time. I mean, he is my man now, so why not leave some of my shit at his house.

Romeo sent a text letting me know he was pulling up. I went to Dreia's room to let her know I was leaving for the night, but she was fast asleep. I guess eating all the good food put her ass in a coma. If she woke up looking for me, she would call. So I decided to leave her alone and be on my way. The moment I opened the passenger door, the smoke hit me in the face. I should've been expecting it because Romeo always hotboxes when he's riding alone. I don't understand how the hell his lungs can take all that shit. He started laughing as I waved my hand in front of me to clear the smoke.

"My fault, baby." He apologized as he rolled all the windows of the truck down and turned the air conditioning on in attempt to clear out some of the smoke.

"I don't know how you do it, smoking with the windows up. I would fuck around and pass out from being too high," I said as I got inside and fastened my seat belt.

"Jul looking for Dreia. He said he was about to come over here if he didn't hear back from her soon."

"Dreia ass in there knocked out. She ate at our mom's, came

home, and passed out." I informed him so that he could pass the message along to his brother.

"Jul going find out the hard way, cause I ain't about to call and tell his ass shit. You tired or you feel like doing something?"

"Depends on what it is. Nothing with too much, but I don't mind doing something." I wasn't tired, but I really just wanted to head back to his place, fuck, and lay up until we fell asleep.

"Coo, I wanna go see a late-night movie, then we can go back to the crib. Did you bring my plate?"

"Yeah, it's right here." I showed him the plate I was holding in my hand.

"Aww, shit baby. I'm high as fuck. I didn't even pay attention to the plate, I only saw your big ass purse on your arm." Romeo said then proceeded to pull out of my driveway.

Pulling into the parking lot of Easton, I didn't expect it to be so crowded. I guess everyone had the same thing in mind about a late-night movie. Romeo pulled to the valet section of the parking lot and we both exited the car. Romeo reached for my hand and we walked through Easton until we reached the box office to purchase our tickets. Romeo couldn't decide on which movie he was interested in, so I choose for us. *Girl's Trip*. I saw the previews for it a couple times, but I honestly had no clue what the movie was about. I'm not a big movie person, I'm more of a TV show watcher.

As we were heading to the concession stand after getting our tickets, I noticed the light-skinned chick from the all-white party that was all in Romeo's face looking in our direction. I knew the day would come when we ran into one of his groupies, but I wasn't expecting it to be today. I was happy that I stayed up on my appearance because I'd hate to run into any of his old hoes looking all washed up. Being his woman, I needed to match his fly and compliment him whenever I was on his side. Rocking a black rumper with silver accessories, silver slides, and small matching clutch, I was dressed down, but I still was looking good. My hair, brows, eyelashes, and nails were of course slayed.

She kept looking in our direction as if she wanted to say something, but didn't know what to say. Romeo looked over and saw her starting as well but he didn't switch up. He continued to hold my hand and walk with me like he never saw her. As long as he didn't show any signs of anything, I could care less about her and her friends looking in our directions because that's what comes with being the woman of Romeo Jones.

Romeo ordered some nachos with cheese, Reese's pieces, and an Icee all from himself. I knew he had the munchies because we originally planned to eat once we got inside of the theater. The dine-in theater has a nice selection of real food to order from and that's what I planned on eating. Heading to the theater our movie was showing in, we walked pass ol' girl and her little group of friends.

I'll be damned if the moment we found our seats and got comfortable, did these trolls come strolling in the theater being all loud. What are the chances that they would be here to watch the very same movie as us? I'm sure they saw us walking into the theater because they for damn sure followed us with their eyes. You can always tell when someone is being extra or doing something for attention and that's exactly what ol' girl and her friends were doing. When you know better, you do better, and it's obvious these hoes had no home training. I'm sure they are all over the age of twenty-one, so why come in here acting like a bunch of fucking kids?

Romeo pressed the button for the attendant to come so we could place our orders from our seats, and the gentleman came over to our seats right away. I placed an order for some hot wings and French fries and Romeo ordered the same. The movie started, and we reclined our seats. One thing about the dine-in theater, it's very comfortable and much better than the traditional movie theater seating. Had I reclined my seat back any further I would've drifted off to sleep.

The food came out and we enjoyed our meal over the movie. I'm glad I picked the movie *Girl's Trip* because it was hilarious. I didn't think Romeo would be engaged with the movie, but he was enjoying it was well and laughing at certain parts. I would definitely need to come back with my sisters and watch this on one of our days we chill together.

As the movie was getting ready to end, Romeo and I decided to exit before the crowd so we wouldn't be stuck in the commotion of all the people. It's like the moment we stepped out of the theater, that's when I smelled bullshit coming in our direction. I could feel it in my gut.

"Hey, Romeo baby!" I heard coming from someone behind us. The voice sounded like the light-skinned chick he used to deal with. I wasn't sure, because I had only heard her at the party that night, but I when I turned around my assumptions were correct.

"Excuse me?" I said, and Romeo stood in front of me and put his arm out as if he was telling me to chill.

"I got this, baby!" he said and stepped in the direction of the chick.

"I thought that was you earlier, but I didn't know for sure." She slurred. That bitch was lying. She knew damn well it was him earlier, she just needed that liquid courage. I'm not the messy type, but I'd be damned if a bitch disrespects me, especially when I ain't did shit to disrespect her.

"Nah Shedeia, you knew it was me, but you knew better. You got a few drinks in you now, so you feeling some type of way. But I'm going warn you now, this ain't what you want. If you see me with my woman then you need to respect that shit. Don't come out of pocket on no funny shit callin me out in public. I'm not your baby and the shit you trying to do is uncalled for. I'mma leave it at that and you enjoy your night." Romeo said and turned to walk away, but not before grabbing my hand.

My blood had started boiling and a part of me wanted to beat the fuck outta that bitch, but I let Romeo handle it. I'm going to try my hardest to put my attitude on ice, but that bitch barked up the wrong tree. There's a time and place for everything, and this wasn't it. Classless ass females like Shadeia, or whatever the fuck her name was, are the exact reason why niggas are uncomfortable with taking their woman out. Because their past just can't let the fuck go. Like, move on already.

As soon as we got the car from valet, Romeo sparked the blunt. His nerves must've been on edge just like mine were. I had never witnessed Romeo get upset, but today when he turned red and the vein in his forehead started throbbing, I knew she pushed one too many buttons with him. Instead of getting on the freeway in the direction of his house he took the ramp going the opposite way.

Smoke with me babe
And lay with me babe
And laugh with me babe
I just want the simple things

Miguel's *Simplethings* played through the speakers as we rode I-270 with no destination in mind. Just vibing and smoking. I couldn't help but think that Romeo showed his emotion and expressed himself through music. It's almost like every song he played with me in the car, I could relate to and felt as if he was playing it just for me. High or not, I knew there was meaning behind the lyrics to the song. After riding for about thirty minutes we began to talk, and Romeo expressed that with me is where he wanted to be. He also said that he would never put me in a situation to look stupid or be laughed at by any other female. He apologized for the shit that Shadeia pulled tonight. I heard just how sincere he was in his tone and I let him know that it was ok. I believed in my boyfriend and I wasn't going to allow the messy bitch cause me to feel any type of way towards him. I told Romeo that no female can change the way I feel about him, only he could do so.

When we finally arrived at Romeo's house, I waited until we were inside, and I turned on Tank's *When We* and began to take control over Romeo. Normally it's him playing music and leading, but not tonight.

NINE

OMAR

Being the oldest of three, I'm always the one they come to when shit
gets real. Normally it's Meo that's ready to jump the gun and get shit
cracking when it comes to the gunplay or war, but not this time. Jul
called me and told me he wanted to meet up because it was time to
handle what Pops talked to us about. I was lost at first because since
the day Pops had that meeting with us, he hadn't mentioned it since.
That was a situation we needed to wait on my father's blessing to
handle. Instead of meeting up with Jul that day, I let it play out and
waited to see if he would mention it again, and he did. So I told him
to meet me at The Slab and call up Meo as well.

Arguing with Destini caused me to be late meeting everyone, and
by the time I got to The Slab, everyone was already having their
drinks and talking.

"Bout time your ass got here. How the fuck you goin call a
meeting and be late?" Jul said the moment I stepped off the bottom
step of the basement, where we met up most of the time.

"Man, women! That's all I'm goin to say!" I ain't feel like getting
into what was the reason behind me being late. I was here to discuss
some'n far more important.

"Ok, so your brothers tell me they are ready to take care of Ramaro's sons now. How do you feel about this? I hadn't heard anything further on him changing territories, so I was allowing it to die down. But what do you think?" Pops questioned me.

"Fa real, I don't know. What's the rush on handling them now, if you haven't heard anything more?" I was lost on why they were so ready to handle things, especially Jul.

"They've been doing their homework and discovered a few things, unlike you I see. What's going on Omar? Have you gotten too comfortable? Whether I spoke on it again or not, you still should've done some homework on the names I gave you." Pops looked at me with disappointment in his eyes. It wasn't that I got too comfortable, but I'd been so focused on making money and shipments I hadn't been thinking about no drama. Shit, we earned our stripes early on, before we claimed the throne, so I didn't think this was really going to be a big issue. Muthafuckas will cross their own parents before they cross us, so I honestly think that once them niggas discover who we are, they won't want any smoke.

"No, not at all. What was discovered?" I asked looking at both of my brothers. Meo took his bottle to the head and Jul prepared to speak while he let the smoke escape his mouth.

"So, the other day while I was talking to Dreia about her ex and some foul shit he said to her that was supposed to be a threat but ain't nothing to worry about, I asked her his name. She told me the niggas name was Kamar, so the light went off in my head when Pops told us them niggas' names. Come to find out the nigga been under our nose and radar all this time. Of course, I did my research on the name Kamar. Come to find out that's the nigga K.R.'s real name."

My mouth damn near dropped when he said that shit. We had been doing business with that nigga for years. I never had any issues with him, but Meo always said he didn't like the nigga's vibe and now I see the reason why.

"I never liked that nigga and I told y'all that. Something about his vibe ain't coo. That nigga probably knew who we were all this time. I wouldn't put it past him. Snake ass muthafucka." Meo fumed.

"He could, but then again he might not. Last Ramaro knew, we lived in Texas and only did business in Ohio. But shit, who knows, I don't put anything past him. However, since Kamar is close and near, he may be the first that needs to be handled just because," Pop said and all I could do was nod my head. I see now why the meetup Jul requested the first time was so important. We had to have this meeting before the next shipment was to go to K.R.. This shit got my head spinning.

"What y'all wanna do?" I asked, not anyone in particular.

"What the fuck you mean what we wanna do? That nigga gotta go. No questions asked." Meo said before taking his bottle of Patrón to the head again.

"I mean nigga, I know that much. I'm saying when and how we going do this?" I fumed back at his hothead ass.

"Shit, I'm trying to take care of this sooner than later." Jul said.

"I agree, Julian. The sooner the better, because if we waste any more time, he may be after one of you or your empire." Pops said in a serious tone.

"Not tonight, but this weekend when everybody out kicking it, we need to handle it. That way, when the next shipment comes in, we straight to the money and nothing else." Jul said.

"Bet. I'm wit the shit!" Meo said as he finished off his bottle. I don't know how that nigga drinks Patrón straight like it's water. I'm surprised his damn liver can handle it. I swear he smokes or drinks far more than he eats. Then to top it off, the nigga don't eat healthily.

We sat around and begin to formulate a plan on how to handle K.R. so that the message would be sent back to his bitch ass father and still keep us off the radar. My pops informed us he wanted to handle his brother personally and would be making a visit to Haiti once his sons were dealt with. Pops retired from the game years ago with the drugs and killing, but I guess it was time for him to step out of retirement to handle this. Pops said that once his sons were dealt with, it would make the beast come out of Ramaro, and that's exactly the state he wanted him in when he finally came for him. He felt like it was long overdue to handle his brother. I agree, because if any nigga disrespects and came for my throat the way my so-called uncle came for my dad, I would have been taken care of him.

Getting home and relaxing my mind was all I wanted to do after today's activities played through my head. I had so much shit hit me all at once I couldn't do shit besides get high and calm my nerves. Destini called me a few times, but I declined her calls. I wasn't in the mood to finish the argument from earlier, especially not right now. I know eventually we would need to talk and conclude what we were talking about earlier, but she needed to sleep on it just as well as I did.

This morning when I woke up, I found Destini going through my phone, which is how the argument started. She had never gone through any of my personal shit, but I guess she felt the need to now, all of a sudden. The moment I said something to her, she threw the phone at me. She started spazzing out talking shit. I know Destini is a firecracker, but she had never talked to me the way she did earlier today. I don't like that disrespectful shit she was saying. I'm not used to a woman coming at me out of pocket, so of course, I put her in her place but that ain't stop her mouth from going.

Destini said my phone kept going off, so she wanted to know who it was and what was so important. Come to find out it was a text message from a chick name Jordan I was fucking with when Tini and I first started fucking around. I guess the chick is pregnant and due to have the baby here sometime soon. It was possible for Jordan to be pregnant by me, because at a point in time I was fucking her just as much as I fuck Tini now, and without protection. Shit, had she not got to acting stupid, I probably would've still been fucking with her.

I'm not the type of man to lie on my dick nor lie about what I did, so I told Tini it was possible and that I did used to fuck with Jordan. Of course, that shit was like throwing shit in her face because I was truthful about not only fucking her, but another woman during the same time period at a point. Shit, we never gave what we have a title, so she's lucky that I only fuck her now. I'm a free man to do what I please until I settle down. I choose not to fuck multiple chicks at once out of respect for Destini, but if she wants to dwell on the past that's her problem to deal with. Women come and go, no I'm not saying I want to let go of her, but I'm not about to go through the motions over some shit I can't change.

I didn't get around to texting or calling Jordan back about the information she sent me, but I planned on it. I needed to know what the hell was going on with her. If the baby was mine she had some explaining to do, because that's something she should've told me the moment she found out, instead of waiting until the baby is almost here. I'm a man, and it's my responsibility to be in my child's life. Whether it's here or not, I need to do what I'm supposed to. Providing for and supporting my child would be a priority of mine and Jordan was depriving me of doing that by waiting so long to tell me.

The more I thought about my situation, the higher I got, and before I knew it I was passed the fuck out sleep. The sleep I got must have been well-needed, because had I not heard someone banging on my front door, I wouldn't have wakened up from my slumber. I grabbed my phone to check the time and noticed I had thirty missed fucking calls. I didn't even check to see who they were from, because whoever was at the door was ringing the bell and banging at the same time.

"HOLD ON!" I yelled in the direction of the front door as I rushed to see who it was. Swinging my front door open, seeing Tini standing there with rage in her eyes, I couldn't do anything besides shake my head. I couldn't believe the side of her I was seeing after so long.

"What the fuck has got into you?" I questioned as I let her inside.

"What the fuck do you mean what the fuck has got into me? The question is what the fuck has got into you. I been calling you since we separated yesterday, and you have yet to answer one fucking call. Then to know some of my calls you sent to voicemail intentionally only pisses me off more. If you couldn't answer my call, why wouldn't you at least call me back?"

"Listen Tini, I'm not trying to start my day how we started yesterday. I'm not about to do this petty ass shit with you. I don't know who the fuck you think you're talking to or dealing with, but I'm not them. You may have been able to get away with this shit in the past with your old niggas, but again I'm not them, and you ain't about to talk to me like I am."

"Fuck outta here with that bullshit. It ain't about who I'm used to and who you are. When I'm played for a fool, I'm going to speak my fucking mind. I have every fucking right to. If you thought you were just going to pull some fuck shit and switch up on me without me speaking the fuck up you got the wrong fucking bitch."

"Destini, I'm trying my hardest to no disrespect you, but you pushing the fuck outta my buttons right now with your mouth."

"Oh, so now you're trying to not disrespect me. But you weren't thinking about that shit when you were running around sticking your dick in random bitch while fucking me, though. You didn't think about the respect you had for me when you got that bitch pregnant either, were you."

"You saying that shit like I knew she was pregnant. I didn't find out until yesterday, so calm all that out. Then to think about all this respect shit you talking, you act like we were serious in the beginning. Shit, I don't know what the fuck you were doing with your pussy in the beginning. For all, I know you could've been fucking around, too. Be thankful that I was honest and at least I did cut the bitch off at some point. We ain't have no title then, and we don't have a title now."

"Oh ok. I see what it is. Say no fucking more. So, since you ain't know what I was doing with my pussy, then don't worry about what I do with my pussy now, since there no TITLE!" Tini said and stormed out of my front door. She rushed to her car and skirted off all fast like a fucking bat out of hell.

The shit she just said to me made me want to break her fucking jaw, but I'm not a woman beater. It only made me wonder what type of shit she was about to be on. I'm not one for chasing behind no bitch, so I'mma give her some space and let her cool down before I talk to her. Destini's mouth gone get her fucked up. That's the problem with women, they always wanna lash out when the mad and say shit without thinking. I hoped like hell I ain't have to fuck Destini up for doing no stupid shit. A woman can't get revenge with her pussy, that's just hoe shit and it's no way around it.

Grabbing my phone, I begin to scroll through all those missed called and noticed they were only from Jordan and Destini. Had it been one of my brothers, I would've been pissed cause we got too much going on for me to miss any of their calls. Since I had already talked to Tini, now I needed to face the music and finally call Jordan back.

"Hello?" Jordan answered the phone after only the first ring.

"What's up?"

"You tell me, I sent you a text message yesterday, only to get the third degree from some female you're dealing with. Then to top it off, I never got a call, text, or anything back from you."

"I called you just now, didn't I?" I didn't have time to be going back and forth with Jordan now. This shit is just getting ridiculous.

"Yeah after I blew your phone up. It shouldn't take all of that for you to finally respond to me."

"Come on now Jordan, I didn't call to argue with you about how many times you called and when I decided to call you back. What I wanna know is how far are you and why the hell you just now telling me something like this?"

"I'm due in three weeks. I didn't tell you because when I found out, I wasn't sure if I was keeping it or not, and by the time I decided I wanted to keep it, I didn't have any other options."

"Ok, you could've told me then. That's a bunch of bullshit. I can't help but think you were on some sneaky shit with this baby situation. I mean what type of woman hides the entire pregnancy from the father until the baby is damn near here. What are you having? Is this baby mine for sure?" I didn't want to get carried away with this baby talk if the baby wasn't for sure mine. But then again whether she said it was for sure mine or not, we were still getting a DNA test done regardless.

"Yes, I'm sure you're the father of the baby I'm carrying. I wouldn't have contacted you if you weren't. I'm not that type of chick Omar, and you know that. I don't want you for what you have, unlike the bitch you're probably dealing with now. I mean, let's be real, how long were we fucking around. I could've been come to you on some fluky shit it that's what was about, but I didn't. I had to allow myself to get over you before I reached out to you. I honestly couldn't handle the fact that you cut me off, for whatever reason, I don't know. But it's over and done with now." Jordan explained and she low key made me feel bad.

I always imagined being married and settled down with the woman who would birth my kids. I'm not the baby momma drama type of guy. I don't want the back and forth relationship with a child in the middle. I grew up part of my life with both parents, and then for the remainder of the years I was left with only my pops. I don't want my child to feel how I felt, nor go through what I did with the transitions of not living in a two-parent household.

"Where are you at, Jordan? We need to meet up. I need to be up-to-date from this point forward when it comes to this baby. And you still didn't tell me what you were having. Better yet we'll discuss this face-to-face."

"I'm at home. You're welcome to come here, because I honestly don't feel like leaving here."

"Alright, let me get dressed and I'll be over there."

We said our goodbyes and I headed for the bathroom to get my hygiene together, so I could get dressed and head to Jordan's place.

TEN

DESTINI

My emotions have been all over the place for the past couple of days. I don't know if I allowed my feeling to grow too strong for Omar, or was I just pissed that for once a nigga had one up on me. Either way, I haven't had contact with his ass since. I needed to stay away from him until I could control my anger, because if not things were going to be far worse than he ever expected. I don't know what type of woman Omar took me for, but just cause he's a boss doesn't mean I'm going to allow the sneaky shit he does slide. Shit, I'm a boss too, I ain't no fuckin employee. I've been loyal to him since the day we started talking, even without a title, so he should've been the same. I know bitches want him and I'm sure he sees bitches he likes, but if that's the case, don't pretend like we are working towards something if that's not the case. He could've let it be known from the jump he wanted to have his cake and eat it too. I wouldn't have any choice but to respect it or keep it moving. But since he didn't know, I'm sitting around looking stupid.

A baby isn't something you can just pretend doesn't exist. I mean he's right, we weren't together, and we aren't together, but still. I'm not an infant-friendly person, I've never had to be around any infants that close and personal. Shit, truth be told I can't have kids, and I believe that's why I'm hurt behind this. I didn't tell Omar I couldn't have kids because we never discussed it. The only person who knew about the fact of me being infertile was Maris. When I was a kid before Maris adopted us, I was molested by a man at another foster home we lived at temporarily. He molested me for a good six months before we were removed from their home. I felt like God had finally answered my prayers when they came and got us from that hell hole. I never told anyone because he threatened to do what he was doing to me to my sisters as well. I felt like then I was protecting them, but now that I'm grown, I know that was only a scare tactic.

Because of the damage, he had done to my insides at a young age, I was told that I wouldn't be able to have children when I had a surgery in my early adolescent years. I told my sisters the surgery was on my Gallbladder because I was ashamed, and Maris went along with me because she said it was my business to tell others. She told me if I didn't want to tell anyone then that was my decision. Maris respected my choice to keep it private, and up until this point, I never really thought about it. The youth center children filled that void I guess, which is why it didn't cross my mind.

Lately, I hadn't been doing much other than working and going home and enjoying my bottle of wine. Tonight, I finally responded to one of the relatives of a little boy at the center who had been trying to get me to come to shoot pool with him for months. He said that the place was pretty laid back for the most part and it's not all rowdy, so I agreed. I needed to get the fuck out of the house. My sisters were living their lives and still wrapped up with the other two Jones bothers so I didn't want to be the Debbie Downer with my pissy mood toward Omar.

I couldn't decide on the right outfit to wear. I didn't want to over-dress, but I didn't want to dress down, either. I figured since we would be shooting pool wearing a dress or a skirt was completely out of the question. I didn't want to bend over, and my entire ass be on display. Some ripped up style jeans with a low cut black leotard ended up being my choice for the evening. Heels are always my choice of shoe when stepping out, so I decided on some open toe black heels with a gold buckle. A gold choker, a few gold bangles, a pair of gold hoop earrings, and a small gold clutch were the only accessories I wore.

Kenny asked me if I would prefer him picking me up or to meet him at our destination. Since I didn't know him well, I decided on just meeting him there. I didn't want anyone coming to my home that I didn't know personally, especially a relative of the youth center kids. I never know how tonight may end, and I don't need him popping up at my house or anything crazy like that.

When I arrived at the pool hall, I sent him a quick text letting him know I had arrived. To my surprise, he was already there and waiting for me. Checking my mirror, I made sure my lipstick was applied neatly and that there wasn't anything out of place on my face. Grabbing my small clutch and phone, I took a deep breath and prepared myself for this random date I had jumped into.

The moment I walked into the building, I noticed Kenny sitting right by the entrance. He stood to his feet and walked in my direction. This man cleaned up damn nice. Normally when I see him, he's dressed down with sneakers, jeans, and a tee type of shirt. Not tonight. He had on a pair of jeans, but he dressed it up with a collared shirt and some nice loafers. Standing about six-feet tall, about 275 pounds of solid muscle, I could tell the gym was one of his closest friends. His dark brown skin complexion was enticing. He had a set of the whitest teeth I had ever seen in my life. To complement his smile, he had one dimple on the right side. Another thing that was a turn on about Kenny is his body was covered in tattoos. Something about that bad boy look caught my attention.

We wasted no time getting our first game of pool going. Just as he promised, the place was very laid back, not a big crowd, and played some pretty decent music. We talked while shooting pool and the conversation flowed pretty well. After warming up some, we both decided it was time to have a few drinks. A few drinks turned into hours of drinking and shooting pool. I found myself enjoying his company far more than I expected. Of course, after too many drinks, he became touchy and I allowed it. I guess my body was yearning a man's touch since I had been into it with Omar. The attention and chemistry between Kenny and I let me know that I still had it and I didn't need to settle for Omar and his bullshit. Us women tend to second guess or question if we are still what we were prior to a relationship once we walk away, and Kenny gave me the validation I needed.

The pool hall closing was the only reason we decided to leave. Had they been open any later, we probably would've still been inside enjoying ourselves. Kenny asked did I want to grab a bite to eat and I agreed. Instead of us taking separate cars, I rode with him. I don't know what type of man I took Kenny for prior, but he was a lot better off than I expected. Driving a 2017 Audi that was fully loaded, he had to be making some sort of money. When we discussed his occupation, he told me that he was in the process of starting his own company for felons that are released from prison and have a hard time finding employment. In my opinion, this was a great idea. I liked the fact he was trying to better our community just as I was. Not many people give a fuck about anyone other than themselves, but he did.

All the questions I asked he seemed to have just the answers I was looking for. A man with no kids over the age of thirty was my main question. The little boy he brings to the center is his nephew that he helps raise. I knew it wasn't his son, but I also didn't know the direct relation until tonight. Pulling into IHOP, I felt my wine beginning to hit me. I only felt a little buzz, but that car ride did it for me.

We were able to walk inside and straight to a seat without a wait, which I was happy about, because my stomach was beginning to growl. The waitress gave us a few minutes to look over the menu, and by the time she returned with our waters, we were ready to place our orders. I ordered the sirloin tips with eggs and Kenny ordered country fried steak with eggs. The food smelled and looked wonderful, but I couldn't eat more than a few bites before my mind went elsewhere. It's like my body started craving dick more than food, and I couldn't block it or remain focused. Kenny must've sensed that something wasn't right, so he asked the waitress for our check and to go boxes.

The moment we got to the car and headed back to the freeway, I asked him to pull over for a second. We were on I70 east. Being that it was almost three o'clock in the morning, the traffic was extremely slow. Kenny pulled over and placed his hazards on, when I didn't open my door, he looked over at me with confusion written all over his face.

"You ok? I thought you had to throw up or something."

"No, not at all. This may seem random, but we only live once and I'm a firm believer in doing what you feel when you feel it." I replied.

"I can dig that, so what do you feel?"

"I want you to turn the lights off, including the hazards, then turn the car off." I said as I begin to unbutton my jeans and the snap from my leotard. My pussy was purring to be touched and I wasn't going to hold back because we were on our first date. I don't give a fuck about none of that, I'm a grown ass woman who lives to please one person, and that person is me.

Kenny began to undress the moment he saw me undressing. When he pulled his boxer briefs off, I looked over and noticed that he was working with at least a foot of dick. Rock hard standing at attention, the thick veins bulging on his dick made my mouth water. I didn't plan on sucking his dick, but the work of art made me think twice. The moment we were both naked from the waist down I advised him to recline his seat.

Straddling Kenny's lap, I placed one foot on the middle console and the other on the door. I used my right hand to massage his dick as I lowered my body down onto him. The moment I felt like he was completely inside of me, I allowed my body to adjust to his size before making any moves. Kenny gripped my waist and I begin to bounce slowly on top of him. I felt my cream coating his dick as if I had already begun to cum, but I hadn't. As I looked into Kenny's face and he begin to bite his bottom lip to prevent from moaning, I started bouncing harder, making sure my ass slapped his thighs as hard as possible each and every time I came down.

"Fuck Destini, this pussy good as fuck! Ride this dick just like that."

Hearing him encourage me and compliment my pussy only boosted my ego more. I began to wind my hips as I bounced up and down showing off just a tad bit so he would know he wasn't working with no amateur.

"Get up and open that passenger door." Kenny instructed, and I obeyed. When this nigga got out the car on the side of the freeway and walked over to my side, I knew shit was about to get real intense.

"Put your ass facing me and face down."

Being told what to do with the tone he spoke turned me on. The moment I was face down, ass up, I felt Kenny's warm tongue touch the crack of my ass and my back arched instantly. It tooted this fat ass up perfectly for him. Using his tongue to fuck my asshole I felt my orgasm near. Just when I thought the shit couldn't feel any better, he used his two fingers to fuck my pussy hole with one hand and the other reached around and played with my clit. This muthafucka was talented, because he never once took his face out the booty.

My orgasms started coming back-to-back. It's like I couldn't control my body. As loud as my moans were, and as much as I told him I couldn't take any more, he made me go a little further and reach another peak. The perfect arch I started with was no longer possible, my body was too weak.

"Get out!" Kenny demanded. I stepped out of the car with wobbly legs and stood to face him. He pushed me against the car and wrapped my legs around his waist as he rammed his thick dick back inside of me. Wrapping my arms around his neck so I wouldn't fall, I allowed him to pound in and out of me on the side of his car. As the few cars that were in passing rode past us, it intensified the moment. I felt like I was in my own real life porno. The excitement of people watching us fuck helped to make this so much more enjoyable.

"I'm cumming! I'm cumming!" I screamed as I felt my body begin to shake uncontrollably. Kenny slowly laid me in the passenger seat of the car as he jacked himself off until he nutted right there on the side of the car. He walked back around to the driver's side and stepped inside. We both slowly placed our clothes back on, and just like that we were right back cruising on the freeway in the direction of my car.

"Destini, your ass crazy as hell. I would've never thought you wanted to pull over for that. One thing I will say is you got some fire between your thighs. Fuck around and make a nigga wanna wife you and start a damn family." Kenny joked.

"Shut up. I couldn't contain myself. Is that a problem?"

"Hell no, it's not a problem. I like spontaneous shit like that." Kenny said as he licked his lips and looked in my direction. That shit only made my pussy jump just thinking of what he just did with that tongue moments before.

Kenny dropped me off to my car and we said our goodbyes. I promised to text him once I got home before starting my car to leave. The entire ride to my place I couldn't stop thinking of the shit I just did. I was so in the moment I didn't even use any protection. First thing tomorrow morning, my ass is going straight to the doctor's office before I head to work. My legs were still a little shaky when I got home. As bad as I wanted to get in the shower before bed, I couldn't muster up the strength, so I passed out right there on my couch, juicy pussy and all.

ELEVEN
DEJA

I don't know what the hell was the purpose of this bitch finding a way to contact me. I thought the night we saw her pressed ass at the movies and Romeo checked her it would be the end of things, but I guess not. Shadeia just couldn't leave well enough alone. If she knew what was best for her, she would beat it before she gets beat the fuck up! I normally don't allow people to follow me on Snapchat unless I know them personally, but lately I haven't given two fucks just allowing anyone and everyone to follow me. Plus, I'm trying to expand my promoting and the following base, so that when the time is right for me to get my club, people know about it.

There wasn't a picture on the bitch's snap and her name was mizzfuckya, so I assumed she was just another random follower. Come to find out the bitch was looking and waiting for me to post some shit, so she could slide in my fuckin inbox. Shadeia got the right idea, but wrong bitch. When it comes to mine, I ain't going. Romeo and me ain't have no issues thus far, but I ain't about to allow no funny shit to take place either. I mean I know they were involved with each other or fucking around before me, but I didn't think they were still in contact.

Earlier I posted a few snaps of Romeo and I in the Camaro clowning around with the dog filter. Then I posted one of him singing Miguel's *Sure Thing* to me, which is the one she replied to with a message. The first part of her message I read was, "aww how cute....." then she went on to say how he sang the same song to her. I ain't give two fucks about him singing to the next bitch because my baby could sing his ass off. What pissed me off was the fact she said that she assumed we were over with or just friends because they just fucked. She didn't say when, but it had to be recent for her to come at me about it.

Already having a couple drinks in my system, I was buzzing. But when I called Romeo and he didn't answer only made me think if he was with her now. No matter what time I call or text him, he replies. So being ignored only caused me to assume the worst. Luckily, I didn't have my car at Romeo's house or I would've left and gone looking for his yellow ass. I don't know where I would begin to look for his ass, but I would've been riding until I found him. Since riding and looking wasn't an option, I went downstairs to where Romeo kept his Patrón stash and opened his bottle he kept tucked away for a rainy day. Instead of grabbing a cup, I opened that bitch and started drinking straight from the bottle.

Before I knew it, I looked up and the fucking bottle was damn near gone. Listening to the very same song Romeo sang to me on the boat that day we made it official, I had completely zoned out. How the fuck could he sing a song claiming that the pimp in his ass died, if he was still fuckin around with bitches? Classless ass trash type bitches at that.

Calling Romeo one more time only to go to voicemail only enraged me. I headed straight upstairs to his bedroom and begin to grab every outfit I could. On a rampage, I begin to throw as many clothes into his bathtub as I could fit. I even grabbed a few pairs of his shoes. When the bathtub was filled with clothes, I made sure the stopper was down and turned on the water. I went back downstairs to retrieve the little bit of Patrón that was left while the tub filled with water. I couldn't decide if I was going to bleach the shit or just let it sit in the water. Either way, it would be a mess for Romeo to clean up and not myself.

By the time I got back upstairs, the tub had overflowed with water. I rushed to shut the water off and left that shit sitting right in there. Sitting on Romeo's bed I wanted to tear some more shit up, but I couldn't decide where to start so I finished the little Patrón that was in the bottle and grabbed my phone to finally reply to Shadeia's message that started all this frustration.

Me: *So, what did you hope to get outta sending me a message?*

Shadeia: *I get what I want outta Romeo, so the only purpose of my message was to inform you of "OUR" nigga's doing.*

Me: *That's cute "OUR NIGGA" huh?*

Shadeia: *Yep you read that shit right. Let me ask you this, where is he at right now?*

Reading that message hurt like hell cause I honestly didn't know where my supposed to be nigga was. For all I know, he could really be with her right now. I hopped like hell he wasn't, but I didn't know and at the rate things were going I wasn't about to find out, because he wasn't answering any of my calls or returning them. Deciding to just send her a message back so I wouldn't look as stupid as I felt, I hoped she didn't come back with anything more.

Me: *Not with you!*

After sending her a message, I powered off my phone. I didn't want to read another thing she had to say. The fucked up part about Snapchat was the messages delete after looking at them so I didn't even have any proof. I didn't screenshot them because she would then know he wasn't with me because I was saving them for a later time. With the many thoughts clouding my mind, I laid there on the bed wondering what the fuck had I got myself into.

Rolling over, I was surprised by the sun shining brightly in my face through the bedroom window. Looking to my left and right I realized Romeo wasn't next to me on either side. The first thought popped into my head was, *I can't believe this nigga ain't come home, to his own fucking house.* I tried to sit up to find my phone and felt the vomit coming up. Rushing to the bathroom I damn near slipped and busted my ass on the wet floor. Looking around seeing water and wet clothing everywhere I wondered what the fuck happened in here.

The last thing I remembered from last night was the bitch Shadeia messaging me and having a few shots of Patrón. It's obvious I had more than that because my fucking head is pounding, and I'm face down in the toilet bowl. After throwing up, dry heaving and spitting up everything that was left inside of me, I finally stood to my feet to brush my teeth and wash my face off. *WHAT THE FUCK?* I thought to myself as I read the large mirror above the bathroom sinks.

STUPID BITCH

Looking down on the counter I noticed my favorite MAC lipsticks smashed as if they were used to write on the fucking mirror. I couldn't believe Romeo would be so fucking childish to use my expensive ass makeup to write on the mirror, and for what. Shaking my head, I turned to start cleaning up the wet clothes off the floor. Picking up drenched clothes that not only belonged to Romeo, but myself as well, I wanted to scream. Wracking my brain to figure out what the fuck happened and how this happened only frustrated me even more. I didn't know if Romeo did this or I did. Either way, it was stupid to include our personal clothes unless we were both at war with each other last night. I don't remember shit. Whatever happened between us two must've pissed him clean off because he's never disrespected me and to call me a bitch was a bit much.

Once I got all the wet clothing from the floor, I placed them in the washing machine on spin cycle, so I could wring them out first before placing them in trash bags to take to the dry cleaner. I refused to wash or dry any of his expensive clothing in fear I may ruin them. Instead of mopping up the wet floor, I used a towel to dry up the water that was left since it wasn't very much.

Completing the cleaning of the water mess, I looked for my phone and realized it was powered off. I never let my phone die or turned it off. I hate that my entire night is a blur and I don't remember anything. The first person I tried to call was Romeo because I needed some understanding of what the fuck was going on between us two and talk to him about the messages I received about him.

Romeo answered on the second ring.

"Oh, so you sober now or you just waking up?" he questioned without a simple hello or good afternoon.

"I'm both. I'm the one who should be asking the questions here. Where are you at? I woke, and you weren't in bed and there aren't any signs that you even slept in the bed with me."

"You damn right I didn't sleep in the bed with you. Did you see the fucking mess you made in the bathroom last night drunk?" Attitude was laced all in his tone.

"Wait so those clothes that were in the tub, I put them there? Oh, my goodness Romeo, tell me you're lying." I placed my head in my hands because I couldn't believe I pulled a stunt like that. I know just how much his clothes cost so trying to destroy them was beyond petty. Fucked up thing is some of my shit was included. Yeah, I had to be drunk, I would've never done no shit like that sober.

"Fuck you mean tell you I'm lying. Shit, I wish I was. Why the fuck would you get so drunk you don't know what you're doing. Then to top it off, why the hell would you try to mess my shit up. That shit is stupid as fuck!" I could hear the tone in his voice getting higher and high. He was pissed and there was no way around it. Shit, I was pissed too. No that wasn't a good enough reason to do what I did without finding out the truth, but in my defense, I don't remember doing it.

"Calm down, Romeo! You getting real hostile for no reason. I did do some fucked up shit, but you fucked up all my got damn makeup too. What was your excuse for that?"

"You should be happy that's all I did! Shit, the whole bathroom was wet last night when I came. With thousands of dollars of shit soaking wet. I don't even want that shit no more it's probably going to smell like fuckin mildew."

"It's not goin smell like mildew. I'm bout to take it to the dry cleaners now."

"Nah, fuck all that shit. I'll get new shit. The damage is already done. Then your sloppy ass was passed out with the fuckin bottle in your hand empty like you were drinking away some fuckin sorrows or something."

"Shit I felt like I was. Your bitch decided to hit me up last night on Snapchat and every call of mine went unanswered, but she somehow knew where the fuck you were."

Just how he was amped up, he was getting me there just thinking about him cheating on me while I'm at his house waiting on him to get home. The fuck did I look like, a fool?

"Are you fuckin serious, Deja. What bitch? I have one woman and that's you, so what the fuck are you talking about?"

"The bitch Shadeia, that's who!"

"Man, get the fuck outta here. I wasn't with no bitch last night. I ain't answer your calls or call you back cause I was in the middle of handling business and I knew I was coming home after. You sound real fucking STUPID right now!"

"No, you sound stupid. Business or not it's not like you just started this business. You do the same work now as you did when we first started. Yet last night was the first night you decided you didn't want to answer the phone, but you do any other time. Prove to me you weren't with that bitch, how about that!" I screamed in the phone

"Deja you about to make me say some shit I'mma regret! All business ain't the same, and if you knew the fucking type of man you with, you wouldn't even be acting so got damn childish. I'mma call you back cause you pissing me the fuck off!" Romeo ended or call before I could even say anything else. A part of me wanted to believe him because he was too pissed. Then again, niggas get mad when they're caught too.

Instead of taking his clothing to the cleaners like I originally planned, I just bagged them all up and tossed them in his dumpster. He wanted to be an asshole and stubborn talking about throw them away he'll replace them, so that's exactly what I'm doing. I should've left that shit in the water in the bathroom.

I grabbed my shit that wasn't wet and got the fuck outta his house. I got a whole place of my own, ain't no need to sit around his. That's the difference between me and the other bitches he deals with, I'm not about to be his bitch. Now his woman, I will be, but not his bitch.

TWELVE
ROMEO

"I ain't never felt this way about no bitch and Deja got me real life fucking tripping. I know she was drunk, but damn she was doing too fucking much. I can't believe she really took and filled my fucking jacuzzi tub with not only my clothes but some of hers as well. When I came in and saw all the soaking wet clothes everywhere. I could've beat her ass right then and there." I vented to my brothers and Pops.

"Nigga but did you really use her makeup to write STUPID BITCH on the fuckin bathroom mirror. No, I take that back YOUR bathroom mirror, nigga. That was a bitch move." Mar said while laughing. I ain't find shit funny.

"Nigga, I couldn't think of shit else to do I was so fucking mad. Shit, the little bit of clothes she does have at my crib were wet right along with my shit, so I took what I knew she cared about and spent her money on and destroyed it."

"Brah, I wish I could've been there to see the look on your face when you saw that shit. Let Dreia try some fuck shit like that, and I can promise you I'mma smack fire out her ass. I don't give a fuck what morals I go against, that's just disrespectful on another level," Jul was telling a muthafuckin lie.

"Get the fuck outta here. Dreia got your ass wrapped around her finger, you ain't about to smack fire outta shit. She don't even look like the type that will fight your ass, let alone allow you to smack her." Mar said.

"She ain't, but if she ever did that shit Deja pulled with Romeo, she gone turn into the fighting type. Cause I'm for sure going to put my hands on her. Especially if she only doing some stupid shit like that off of assumptions."

"My fucking point! Dej should know we better than that to allow that bitch Shadeia to get in her ear about anything. Shadeia knew what she was doing when she saw Dej out with me the first time. She should've just kept going on about her fucking life instead of trying to start some shit for no reason. I ain't touched that bitch since I made it official with Dej."

"Now that's something I can't believe, son!" Pops finally spoke.

"Na, I swear Pops, I been faithful as fuck. I shock the hell outta myself sometimes when I think about the shit. But I ain't got no reason to cheat. Deja fills all the roles I would need any other woman to fill, so there's no need," I confessed.

"Some of us get to that point where we are ready to settle down and leave these chicks in the streets alone young, and some of us don't. I thought your ass was for sure going to roam the streets well into your thirties. I tell you one thing, I'll be happy when one of y'all make me some grandbabies." I knew Pops was getting around to that, and soon. He always slides that in somewhere.

"Shit, at this rate I don't know if I can handle Deja pregnant. If her emotions got her like this without being pregnant, I can only imagine how the fuck she might show out carrying my seed."

"Yeah, nigga you met your match. That's all that is." Mar said and laughed. That nigga had some nerve cause he met his match as well dealing with Destini. She is a fuckin firecracker and I peeped that shit the moment I met her.

I stayed at The Slab chopping it up with them for a couple of hours until I calmed all the way down. Smoking a couple of blunts and a bottle a Patrón was all I needed to get my nerves back right.

Just as we were the night before tonight we went riding to handle the niggas Kamar, or K.R., whatever you wanna call him, and Kenneth. Had Deja given me the time to explain to her before she had a fuckin tantrum, she would've known it wasn't drug business I was handling. Whenever guns are involved, I don't allow the distractions of a phone to interfere. Shit, none of us do. But you ain't see Dreia or Destini acting a fucking fool. Deja really showed her age with this stunt. I forgive her because I do love that woman, but I needed to handle this family feud first.

We had been waiting discreetly outside of K.R.'s spot for about an hour waiting for everyone to leave besides him and Kenneth. Omar felt if we waited until everyone was gone, it would be fewer witnesses and fewer people to get rid of. I agreed. The fewer bodies we had to drop, the easier it would be. We didn't need it to become a bloodbath of any sort, so our best option was to wait.

The moment the last car pulled off for the night, I noticed Kenneth do his walk around the premises to verify shit was coo. Once he walked back in, we stepped out of the all-black Ford F-150 and headed in the direction of the house. With .32, .44 and AR15's in hand, we were ready to start this war. Creeping up on the old porch we all looked at each other before Omar made the move.

"1, 2, 3..." I counted, and Omar kicked the front door.

BOOM!

With one kick, the flimsy wooden front door went flying in. I didn't notice anyone in the first room where K.R. normally is posted but I'm sure they heard our entry.

"You muthafauckas want a war huh?" I heard a voice say and shots started ringing out from both directions.

I swear there were so many gunshots you would've thought the US army was inside this house. When all fire stopped, the air was full of gunsmoke. It was hard to make out who was who. I noticed two bodies lying in pools of blood and I heard Jul call my name. Temporarily, I had blacked out.

"Meo, let's go! Mar hit, nigga!"

Hearing Jul tell me that my big brother had been hit snapped me into reality. Rushing in the direction of Jul and Mar, all I could see was blood leaking from Mar at a rapid rate. Helping Jul to pick Mar up, we rushed to the truck. Mar wasn't talking and he appeared to be hit more than once. It wasn't hard to believe because the niggas came from two different directions as if they were waiting for us to come in that bitch. Even with a bulletproof vest, he managed to get hit. I couldn't tell where he was hit because he was covered in blood. The only thing on my mind was getting him to the nearest hospital.

If I lost my brother, I don't know how I would handle things. It's always been us three and I can't see life no other way. I immediately grabbed my phone to call Pops to let him know we were headed in the direction of the hospital.

"Pops, Mar got hit! I don't know where, but he's hit. He's bleeding out fast!"

"GET HERE! GET HERE NOW!" Pops demanded before ending the call. I was in such a shock I really was about to make the mistake of actually taking my brother to the hospital. I made a U-turn in the middle of the street and headed to The Slab. By the time we got there, I'm sure Pops would have the proper people awaiting our arrival. Going ninety miles per hour the entire ride, the only thing I could do was say a silent prayer that my brother made it.

When I pulled up to The Slab, there were several people outside waiting for us. They wasted no time getting Mar out of the car and rushing him into the house. My Pops was standing outside waiting for us as well.

"How did this happen?" He questioned Jul and me.

"It's almost like they were waiting for us. They came from two different directions of the house and we didn't realize Mar had been hit until the shots came to an end." Jul explained.

"Y'all are too smart for this. This isn't something new! You were raised in this shit!" Pops said and walked inside the house. He headed straight for the basement. I wasn't sure where they took Mar, but I noticed the trail of blood going int the direction of one of the master bedrooms near the kitchen.

I couldn't follow the trail because I didn't want to see my brother like that. Heading to the basement to join Pops, Mar and I both were silent. I don't know if it was guilt or fear, but we were both speechless. I headed straight for the bar in the corner to grab the bottle of Patrón. Jul was already in the process of rolling him a blunt while drinking 1738 from the bottle. Pops even had him a cup of something dark. I didn't know what it was, because it's obvious he poured it before we got here. His eyes were bloodshot red. He kept speaking in Haitian Creole and saying something over and over. We never learned to speak the language, so I couldn't make out what the fuck he was saying.

An hour passed, and we still didn't have any update on Mar. Pops had gone upstairs several times but didn't have any updates for us. While waiting for some sort of news, I called Deja to tell her what happened. I also wanted her to get in contact with Destini so she could inform her. I forgot all about being upset with her. That shit was minor right now compared to what I was faced with at the moment.

Deja called me back and said she was on the way with her sisters and mom. Right now, I needed her near more than ever and I'm sure my brothers felt the same way about her sisters. Deja was my peace, which was exactly what I needed at the moment. The alcohol and weed didn't seem to be kicking in, nor taking any type of effect on my mental state calming down. I don't know if it was because of my adrenaline or tolerance being so high. Either way, it wasn't good. Deja text me letting me know she was pulling up and I headed upstairs to let them in.

Jul came upstairs right as the ladies we walking inside. Deja walked in first, following her was Dreia. Destini came strolling in last hysterical. She was being comforted by an older woman who looked real familiar, but I couldn't see her face clearly because she wasn't facing me.

"WHO THE FUCK INVITED HER TO MY HOME?" Pops yelled as he walked into the front room.

At that moment, the older woman looked up and that's when array of flashbacks hit me! All the ladies' eyes were on Pops and our eyes were fixed on them.

Pops began to rush in the direction of Destini speaking Haitian Creole and before Jul could stop him...

TO BE CONTINUED!

Stay tuned for part two!

SNEAK PEEK

Tasha NiCole of Magnificent Pens Presents...
Untitled

Growing up in Columbus, Ohio, Don'Ray Banks, the king of Columbus, was a big-time drug dealer. Standing tall at six-foot-one, built of two hundred thirty pounds of steel, he was quite the eye catcher. To say he was attractive would have been an understatement. His skin tone was flawless. Zantina would say his skin resembled a pot of hot melted caramel, and all the ladies wanted to dip their apples in it. He started losing his hair at an early age due to heredity. He rocked a bald head with a full beard. Don'Ray had strong, dark, but seductive features, with thick eyebrows and long eyelashes. He sort of puts you in the mind of Tupac, just taller and a lot bigger.

When Zantina met Don'Ray, she was working as a medical assistant while continuing her education to become an RN. She had no intentions of getting involved with anyone, let alone settling down. She wanted to have all her ducks in a row before making a family. Unfortunately for her, Don'Ray was irresistible—not just his appearance, he had that Casanova charm. No woman was able to escape his ability to attract and seduce them right into his bedroom. Zantina was no exception.

Don'Ray saw something different in Zantina, more than he saw in all the other women he ever encountered. Although he eventually got what he wanted, she made him work for it; his money and reputation didn't make her give up the goodies any quicker. Zantina had only been with one man before meeting Don'Ray, and she had vowed to never sleep with anyone else until marriage. While she couldn't resist Don'Ray's charm long enough to wait for marriage, she made him wait longer than any other female ever had. It didn't take him long to see Zantina was the type of woman he needed to balance out his lifestyle. He knew he needed to lock her down before somebody else did.

Together, they were like Jay and Bey. All the women envied Zantina, and all the men wanted her. She was blessed with a beautiful, golden complexion, and naturally long, jet-black hair. She stood five-foot-three, weighing one hundred and forty pounds, most of which was butt, hips, and thighs. Needless to say, she was just as irresistible as Don'Ray, so they complimented each other. He always said it was her Puerto Rican accent that really attracted him to her. When she'd get mad, she would curse him out in Spanish, but he would just laugh. He once told her that sometimes he made her mad on purpose, just to hear her Spanish accent.

She yelled at Don in Spanish, while walking out of the room. "Tu, usted consequir en, sobre mi de mierda el nervio el pendejo, el ano."

He laughed and looked at his daughter, Beauty, for a translation, which was the only time she had his permission to curse. She laughed and said, "You get on my fucking nerves, asshole." He laughed even harder once he knew what Zantina had said.

Shortly after they married, she became pregnant with Don'Ray Jr. The moment Don'Ray found out she was carrying his child, their bond became ten times stronger, and so did the love and respect he had for her. Besides his mother, she was the only woman Don'Ray had any respect for, that is, until the birth of his daughter. Their union couldn't be torn down with a bulldozer. He made sure she had everything she ever wanted, and he didn't leave out anything! She studied his every need and desire as if her life depended on it—and it did if she wanted to keep him. He had a line of women as long as I-71 waiting for a chance to walk in her shoes, and they were willing to do anything that she wouldn't. That was why their separation came as such a surprise.

They split up in 1992. She left him when their daughter was seven years old, but Don wasn't the only one she left behind. He was forced to become a full-time father overnight. He had to learn to juggle fatherhood and hustling, which were both full-time jobs. He made it look easy, though. He always made sure Beauty's schoolwork was not just done, but done correctly.

Don loved to cook, so they spent a lot of time in the kitchen. Today was no different. Beauty was teaching her dad to make Pulpo a la Gallega, his favorite Spanish dish made with Galician octopus. Her mother used to make it for him. After a taste test, Don closed his eyes, as if he was dreaming, and said, "Beauty, when the time comes, you are definitely going to make some man happy to have you as his wife. This is almost as good as your mother's."

He peeked through one eye to see if she was offended by his comment. Once they made eye contact, they both laughed.

Don taught Beauty at an early age how men viewed promiscuous girls, and explained why it was important she avoided that path. She held dear everything her father taught her. He taught her things from a male's perspective; however, he had left it up to her mother to teach her how to be a lady. Beauty even learned a few nursing techniques from her mom because her dad was a diabetic. When her mom was around, she took care of him. Doctor visits weren't necessary. Naturally, it became her responsibility when her mother left. She made sure her dad stayed in good health.

Don'Ray never really spoke of her mom after she left. Beauty could tell he missed her when she would mention her. Truth be told, so did she. Although she was still spending lots of time with her, she missed how things were when they were living together as a family. The only time Don'Ray would really speak about her mom was when Beauty did or said something that reminded him of her. He would just smile and tell her that she was the spitting image of her mother, but she had his eyes and personality.

There weren't any ill feelings toward her mother for leaving her behind. She didn't really have a choice. She knew she would have to kill Don'Ray in order to take his daughter away from him. If he never cared about anything else, she knew for sure that his baby girl, Beauty, was his soft spot. He nicknamed her Beauty because he felt she was God's most beautiful creation. Beauty wouldn't have had it any other way because she knew that she was his sanity.

When Beauty's mom was around, it was a lot easier for Don'Ray to keep business and family separate. No one on the business side had ever seen or heard of Don'Ray's wife and children, so they weren't aware that he had become a full-time father. It wasn't kept a secret because he was embarrassed, it was his way to keep from jeopardizing their safety. There could be a houseful, but no one ever knew Beauty was there. After Zantina left, Don had no choice but to bring business a little more close to personal than he ever thought he would.

Before Beauty was old enough to really understand Don's lifestyle, he would always put toys in his walk-in closet, which was twice the size of a master bedroom in most houses. Whenever he was having company, he would say to her, "Beauty, go to your playroom." He had a remote control that would raise the back wall of the closet, like a garage door, and there were wall-to-wall monitors that displayed every part of their home. He used this space for a playroom because it was soundproof. There was no way of knowing that Beauty, or the playroom, existed unless you were told. Without the remote control, the wall could only be raised from the inside. Don used the closet as his way of keeping tabs. He knew where Beauty was, and he knew that she was safe. He also had a camera connected to his phone, so he was able to keep an eye on her without making it noticeable. He knew that if anything ever happened inside his home, they could kill him, and they'd still never find Beauty.

The older Beauty got, the more attached to Don'Ray she became. She never wanted him to leave her sight. After all, he was all she had and vice-versa. Beauty was just as protective of him as he was of her. At the age of fourteen, she had become fully aware of Don's lifestyle; she also understood the danger that came along with it. Although it scared her at times, she played tough in front of Don because she didn't want him to think she was weak like Zantina.

Zantina left because she couldn't handle Don'Ray's lifestyle. She was ready for him to get out of the drug game. She had been with him through a ten-year bid before Beauty was born. He promised that once he got out that things would change for the better. They didn't. Instead, he got deeper and deeper in the game. Zantina knew there was no chance of him leaving the game anytime soon. When she first left, it was only meant to be a threat. She figured her absence would open his eyes. She left thinking he would come after her, but he never did. Eventually, she moved on with her life, but Don'Ray never did.

Beauty understood that Don'Ray's way of living was the only way he was able to provide her with a life that most children only dreamt of. Once he realized she knew and understood what he did for a living, Beauty was no longer required to go to the closet when company was present. She was still expected to stay out of company's view. However, when guests were over, her protective nature would kick in, and she would go to the closet anyway to avoid being too far away from him in the case something was to ever happen.

Don understood Beauty's fear of not being there to protect him. He didn't have a problem with her wanting to use the closet as her safe place. Instead of him sending her to the playroom, he would say, "Beauty, I've got your back. Now, go watch mine."

She knew that meant company was coming. Don's company had never seen Beauty before, but she recognized every face and voice that ever entered their home. Only people that Don'Ray felt he could trust were welcomed. These were the niggas he trusted with everything, including his life. Regardless of their relationship, he never trusted a soul when it came to Beauty.

Today, like any other day, Don'Ray and Beauty were in the TV room, waiting on the game to come on. Dallas Cowboys vs Pittsburgh Steelers. She wasn't really into football, but she pretended to be, just because it gave her a reason to spend time with her dad. Since the game had not yet come on, she found it to be the perfect time to talk about how she wanted to spend her birthday that coming weekend. For Beauty's eleventh birthday, Don had sent her and Zantina to Paris for two weeks. She cried and cried because he wasn't going to be with them. Every birthday, all she wanted was to spend it with both her parents. He told her because he was a felon, he was unable to get a passport. He wanted her to take lots of pictures to show him when she got back.

After being in Paris for three days, Beauty was ready to go home so she could wake up with her mom and dad on her birthday. Her mom told her they couldn't leave yet. The worst feeling Beauty ever felt was knowing her dad wouldn't be able make it to celebrate her birthday for the first time in eleven years. She knew her dad had ways to make things happen when he wanted to. In her mind, he just didn't want to spend her birthday with her that year. Beauty's feelings were so hurt that she couldn't even enjoy the trip. She ended up falling asleep early.

At exactly 12 AM on the dot, there was a knock at the door. She wasn't really excited to answer it because all she wanted was her daddy; she knew he wasn't coming. By the time she opened the door, roses and candy surrounded her. In the middle was a teddy bear that was the same size as Beauty, holding a heart that said, 'I love you'. She knew it was from her dad, so she smiled, but when she read the card, it was signed by her mom. Not that she didn't appreciate her mom, she was just used to sharing this moment with her dad.

Zantina was asleep. Beauty didn't want to wake her, so she

pushed the cart that held the roses into her room and started to unload it. Just then, the room door opened. It startled her. Then, she heard someone say, "What did I tell you about locked doors, Beauty?" She jumped up so fast and hugged her daddy. That was the best birthday of her life because she was actually surprised.

Based on the past thirteen years of her life, she knew there was no spending limit for her birthday. She had been just about everywhere and had just about everything. This year, she didn't want much, just a shopping trip to LA with both of her parents, without work and interruptions. Just their little family and other family members that lived there. Columbus wasn't a fashion city, so this trip was much needed for Beauty. Everybody shopped at the same places. You had to travel to get exclusivity. She wasn't very materialistic, but she fell in love with fashion watching her dad get fly every day for absolutely no reason. He never wore anything twice. His mother told him cleanliness was next to Godliness, and in his mind, that was what she meant.

"So, Dad, we're still going to Cali this weekend for my birthday, right?" Beauty asked with puppy dog eyes, knowing he wouldn't be able to say no.

"Beauty, I already told you we are doing whatever it is you want to do. You are such a nerd, so worried about a test that you want to sit in this house with me watching football on your birthday. Instead, you could have missed a day of school and started your celebration today. You get that shit from ya mother. I respect it though, which is why you can always have whatever you want, as long as I'm breathing. You spoke to your mother? Is she coming, or is it just us?" Don said.

"I am not a nerd. You're the one that taught me business before pleasure, remember? Anyway, mom said she would come once I figured out exactly what I was doing. I already told Grandma and Grandpa we were coming, though. I had to confirm that you didn't make any other plans. Oh yeah, for the record, you know I don't mind spending my birthday watching football with you. You know you're my favorite person in the world."

She was smiling from ear-to-ear because her dad had agreed to the trip, but before they could discuss any further details, his phone rang. Immediately, Beauty got quiet because the look on his face told her it was a business call. In the midst of his conversation, he pointed towards the closet. She grabbed the remote, opened the closet wall, and made herself comfortable.

IF YOU HAVEN'T ALREADY MAKE SURE
YOU CHECK OUT OTHER WORK BY
CHANIQUE J.

No love given 1-4
Crazy About your love 1-2
No with without you and I 1-2
Fistful of Love (Part 2) Anthology
Loving Everything about my savage 1-2
I need you bad (Standalone)
His weekend lover; loving a boss through it all
Giving my heart and soul to the realist (Spin-off of weekend lover)
A street Queen stole my heart 1-2 (Collab with Tyanna C.)
When a thug pays you in tears (Standalone)

ACCEPTING SUBMISSIONS

Magnificent Pens Presents is currently accepting submissions from aspiring and established authors. Urban Fiction, Street Lit, African American Romance, Romance, LGBT Fiction, Women's Fiction, Christina Fiction, Suspense/Thriller, Erotica, and BWWM are all acceptable genres. If you have a finished manuscript that you would like to submit for consideration email the following: Contact information, synopsis, and the first three chapter in a word document to Magnificentpenspresents@gmail.com

Please allow 2-3 days for a response.

SUBSCRIBE

Text Shan to 22828 to stay up to date with new releases, sneak peeks, contest, and more....